THE WIZARD'S APPRENTICE

Herbie Brennan's work has appeared in more than fifty countries. He began a career in journalism when he was eighteen, and at twenty-four he became the youngest newspaper editor in his native Ireland.

By his mid-twenties, he had published his first novel, a historical romance brought out by Doubleday in New York. At age thirty, he made the decision to devote his time to full-length works of fiction for both adults and children. Since then he has published more than a hundred books, many of them international bestsellers.

The Wizard's Apprentice

YOUR SECRET PATH TO MAKING MAGIC

HERBIE BRENNAN

ILLUSTRATED BY STEPHANIE VON REISWITZ

ff

faber and faber

First published in 2007
by Faber and Faber Limited
3 Queen Square London WC1N 3AU

Edited and designed by Susan Reuben and Sophie Pelham, Baobab
Printed in the UK by CPI Bookmarque, Croydon, CR0 4TD

A CIP record for this book
is available from the British Library

ISBN 978-0-571-23178-2

2 4 6 8 10 9 7 5 3 1

For dearest Dolores,
wizard and priestess, who has
shared the adventure

Contents

1
The Wizards Among Us

Nobody knew why John Clelland travelled to London four times a year. He had no relatives there, no business interests, no close friends. He never stayed long either. Most times he'd fly in one day and fly out the next. And always on the same dates – 21 March, 21 June, 23 September, 21 December.

John was an estate agent. He owned a smallish company that employed seven people. None of them had any idea what he was up to. Even his secretary didn't know why he visited London.

Nobody suspected he was a wizard.

To become a wizard, John trained more rigorously than any athlete. But he wasn't training his body. Each day, seven days a week, without breaks for Christmas, birthdays, holidays or any other celebration, he strove to take control of his *mind*. He followed a routine that included relaxation, breath control, study,

meditation, contemplation and visualisation…
not to mention record-keeping.

The regime was based on an ancient Jewish
mystical system called Qabalah. But it was
Qabalah few rabbis would recognise. It was
overlaid with techniques of Mediaeval magic,
Oriental yoga, pagan practice and secret
Christianity.

The training programme was supervised by
a London-based school of wizardry. Its principles
were centuries, even millennia, old.* The school
never advertised, recruited, or issued a prospectus.
It worked on the belief that when a pupil was
ready, he (or she) would somehow find it.

John Clelland† found it when he was thirty-
eight years old. He believed in magic – real
magic, that is, not the conjuring tricks you see on
stage – and wanted to be a wizard himself. More
to the point, he wanted to meet like-minded
people, who knew what they were doing and
could teach him magic's deepest secrets.

When he applied to join the school, he was
told that his training wouldn't guarantee
admission. For that he had to pass an interview.
How he did in his studies would be taken into
account, of course, but it wasn't everything. It

---

* Its principal, by contrast, was quite young.
† Don't get excited: this isn't his real name.

wasn't even the biggest thing. What really counted was what the school thought of him. The official decision was final. There would be no appeal.

Despite the uncertainty, John decided to go ahead. The school appointed a supervisor to keep an eye on him. Even as a trainee, he would be experimenting with some powerful magical techniques and the supervisor's job was to keep him out of trouble.

The school laid down some ground rules. The lessons would be issued monthly and John had to pay for them. But the sum was so small it barely covered the postal costs, let alone a supervisor's salary.*

He had to agree he would take no mind-altering drugs during his studies. Illegal substances were to be avoided altogether and he was asked to notify his supervisor before taking any prescription medication. He also had to forego all other forms of mystical training, including meditation and yoga, while on his course. The school didn't disapprove of them, but explained that anything that influenced his mind might conflict with his magical training.

John got down to work. He had no way of

---

* Later John learned all the school's supervisors were unpaid volunteers.

knowing that half the school's pupils dropped out after the first few lessons. More still disappeared by the two-year mark. Learning magic sounds glamorous, but it's actually hard, grinding work. Minds don't like to be trained and dream up all sorts of distractions to put a stop to it.

But John persevered. He discovered that his wizardry course was nothing like ordinary school work and even less like the way wizardry is portrayed in fiction. There were no exams, no lectures; there was no face-to-face contact with his supervisor.

Even the way the school judged his work was peculiar. The first lesson a pupil submitted was always marked *adequate*, whatever its standard. After that, every lesson was marked as *adequate*, *adequate plus*, *adequate minus* or *inadequate*. *Adequate* meant it was the same level as the first lesson. *Adequate plus* meant it was better. *Adequate minus* meant it was worse. *Inadequate* meant it was so bad it had to be done again.

It was a cunning system. Every pupil set his or her own standard.

John slogged through. Some of the work was exciting, some of it dull, much of it repetitive. He bought obscure books by obscure writers and waded through a list of recommended reading, much of which left his mind reeling. There were times when all he wanted to do was throw in the towel. But something in him forced him to stick at it and the day finally came when he finished his last lesson.

He waited expectantly, but nothing happened.

After a while, John reread some of his course literature and discovered that if he wanted to go further, he had to make another application to the school. But nobody seemed to care whether he did or not. Some pupils finished the course and left it at that. Others pushed to become full members. It was entirely up to them.* John applied at once.

A week or two later he received a letter asking him to travel to London for an interview. It suggested a date about a month away. John confirmed he'd be there.

The school's headquarters turned out to be a large Victorian terrace house in a quiet, leafy city suburb. As they pulled up, John's taxi driver remarked, 'Must be toffs live here.' There was nothing at all to suggest a school, no brass

* Although this was not entirely clear at the time, John had a third option. Having completed preliminary training, he could have postponed applying until he felt ready to join. There was no time limit. The school kept careful records and held them indefinitely. While it was unusual, some pupils applied for membership years after successfully completing the preliminary course.

plaque, no classroom activity. As the cabby said, it looked like the private home of somebody a bit posh.

John's interview was conducted by two men. Neither went to great pains to explain who they were. One was John's age, possibly a bit younger. The other was substantially older. Both of them were neatly dressed. The younger man was almost entirely bald. Neither would have looked out of place in a city office.

The interview wasn't at all what John expected. It lasted barely twenty minutes and made no reference to wizardry. His work to date wasn't mentioned either. The whole thing was conducted more like an informal chat than anything else. At one point, the younger man asked him casually *why* he wanted to join the school. John hadn't expected that one and took refuge in waffle.

'I'll just put it down as "spiritual itch",' the young man said.

When it was over, John went home feeling depressed. He didn't think he'd done well and neither of the men had given any clue as to his decision. But less than a week later he received a short letter saying his application had been accepted. It then listed possible dates for his formal inauguration.

Except the letter didn't say *inauguration*. The term used was *initiation*. John became aware that he would be known in the school as an *initiate*.

But that was just a fancy name for *wizard*.

* * *

The idea that there are secret schools where you can learn magic goes back a long time.

In 1614, a pamphlet entitled *Fama Fraternitatis* ('Account of the Brotherhood') began to circulate in Germany (and later across Europe). It claimed to speak for a secret society that was the guardian of magical knowledge.

This, and another paper issued two years later, told the story of Christian Rosenkreuz, the young son of poor but noble parents. Rosenkreuz travelled the world in search of wisdom and subsequently joined with three monks to found an Order called the Fraternity of the Rosy Cross.

One hundred and twenty years after he died, a later generation of brethren were making some alterations to a building when they discovered a hidden vault. It was mysteriously illuminated by a sun-like light source set into the ceiling.

The seven-sided chamber contained curious artefacts. There were mirrors with magical properties, perpetually burning lamps, small bells and a manuscript account of the founder's life. Beneath a central altar lay the body of Rosenkreuz himself, still perfectly preserved.

The story gripped a huge audience. The *Fama Fraternitatis* was reprinted three times in 1615 and again in 1617. It quickly went into Dutch and English translations. As a result, large numbers of people throughout Europe were desperate to join the Rosicrucians (as the secret Order was called) to learn the magical arts. Alas, none of the published sources gave any clue how this might be done.

The difficulties did little to dampen the idea that powerful wizards were abroad in the world, practising magic, influencing events and willing to teach their arcane arts to suitable candidates.

During the late eighteenth entury, German Freemasons suggested there were 'Secret Chiefs' behind their Lodge. A century later, an extraordinary Russian named Helena Petrovna Blavatsky claimed to be in contact with 'Hidden Masters' living in the Himalayas. Rumours began to spread of a Great White Lodge, whose near superhuman members were responsible for the spiritual welfare of the planet.

Some hopefuls published their own pamphlets expressing their desire to become Rosicrucians. The idea was that if you printed enough of them, one might find its way into the right hands. At the same time, various organisations appeared claiming to be (or to be descended from) the original Order.

None of these organisations paid much attention to the Rosenkreuz legend until the establishment, in 1888, of the Hermetic Students of the Golden Dawn.

The Golden Dawn was a magical school with a wide-ranging curriculum. Its members included the Irish poet W. B. Yeats, the authors Sax Rohmer and Algernon Blackwood and the actress Florence Farr. They learned the Hebrew Qabalah, elements of astrology, the art of separating their minds from their bodies and the means by which Dr John Dee, Court Astrologer to Queen Elizabeth I, managed to talk to angels.

The Golden Dawn also taught ritual magic. One of its ceremonies took candidates into a seven-sided vault to witness a re-enactment of Christian Rosenkreuz's rediscovery.

Wizards and Witches

In fairy tales and children's books, the term *witch* is often used as if it was the female of *wizard*. In fact, a witch is something else entirely.

Wizards are people, male or female, who practise magic. They can be Christians, Jews, Moslems, Hindus, Buddhists, any other religion or no religion at all.

Witches, male or female, also practise magic (usually) but that's not what makes them witches. They are witches because they are followers of Wicca, the Old Religion of the Goddess and her consort, the Horned God.

The Golden Dawn flourished until the early years of the twentieth century then went into a decline. But before it disappeared, the Order revealed the secrets of its wizardry to a psychic and psychoanalyst named Dion Fortune. She then founded a magical school of her own. It was this school that admitted John Clelland. It continues to train pupils in Qabalah and other secret arts to this day.

* * *

Dion Fortune's school is not the only organisation to teach the ancient practice of magic in our computer age. As a result, there are scattered throughout the world men and women wizards* whose minds work differently to those of other people, who labour to develop strange powers and firmly believe that life is not at all what it seems.

The wizards amongst us have their own agenda, their own interests and their own way of doing things. But most of them practise their wizardry in *secret*. On the face of it they appear to be ordinary men and women, as John Clelland appeared to be an ordinary estate agent.

Which means your next-door neighbour

---

* Despite what you've read in Harry Potter, a female wizard is still called a wizard. A witch is something different. See the panel opposite.

might be a wizard. Your teacher might be a wizard. Even your dear sweet old grandmother might be a wizard.

You might even be a wizard yourself one day. If you're prepared to do the work.

* * *

When Christian Rosenkreuz began to learn the magical arts in 1394, he was barely sixteen years old. Today, most of the secret schools are wary about teaching anyone so young. I was nineteen when I began my training and was initiated on the afternoon of my twenty-fourth birthday, the very earliest moment the school would accept a fully fledged member.

Today, the minimum age is thirty. But however old you are, you can learn some of the things I did, in the remainder of this book.

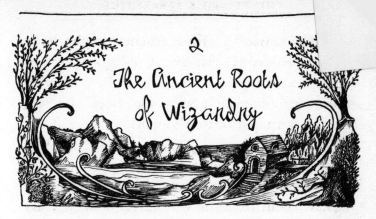

2
The Ancient Roots of Wizardry

There's a magical game you can play, called *Find the Bone*.

To play it, you'll need:

1. Two bones of identical size. Each has to be small enough for you to hide easily in one hand. Wrap a piece of black thread around the middle of one bone so you can tell them apart. The bone you've wrapped is known as the 'marked bone'.

2. Eight identical totems. These can be feathers, pebbles, pieces of crystal or bits of stick.

3. A referee and organiser, who might as well be you since you're the only one who knows the rules.

4. At least twelve players. Fewer if you're stuck, but it's better fun with twelve or more.

5. A coin. (For tossing.)

6. Something you can use to mark out a line

on the floor – chalk, a piece of string or whatever.

Divide your players into two teams. Toss the coin to decide which hides the bone. Let that team appoint a *Hider*, who's going to conceal the bone, and maybe a backup in case the Hider turns out to be useless. The opposing team appoints a *Seer*, the person who's (hopefully) going to find the bone. A backup here could be a good idea as well.

Before play starts, the two teams have to negotiate a wager. This doesn't have to involve money (though it can) but it does have to involve something desirable. They might, for example, agree that the losers will give the winners a massage. Or organise a special party for them. Or cook them a meal. Or loan them a valuable book for a week. Whatever it is, it has to be an incentive to win.

The negotiation is important, so don't rush it. Encourage both teams to decide separately what they're prepared to offer if they lose and what they might settle for if they win. Then bring them together again to hammer out a deal.

When they're ready, mark a line on the ground. Stand the teams on either side of it and give each of them four totems. These should be laid out in plain sight on the team's side of the line. Give the Hider team the two bones. Now explain the rules:

1. No part of a team member's body, including her hands, must cross over the centre line.
2. Once the game starts, nobody except the referee is allowed to say anything.

If anybody breaks a rule, their team loses a totem to the opposing side.

When the game starts – which means nobody can talk – the members of the Hider's team should turn their backs and surround him while he (or she) decides in which hand to hide the marked bone. The unmarked bone is hidden in the other one.

While this is going on, the Seer's team kneels, sits, lies or squats cross-legged in any formation it decides. But they must face the line with their Seer to the front.

When the bones are hidden, the Hider team turns to face its opponents. The Hider steps forward and holds out both hands (making sure they don't cross the line). The Seer then guesses which hand holds the marked bone. If she* guesses right, she earns a totem from the opposing team. The referee is responsible for moving it across the line. If she gets it wrong,

* In my experience the best Seers are female.

one of her team's totems goes to the Hider team.

Lost totems may be won back in the course of the game. The team that successfully collects all eight totems at one time wins.

I know what you're thinking. This game has nothing to do with magic. But that's because I haven't told you everything.

Find the Bone is played *shamanically*. To find the bone, the Seer sends out her *power animal*, a creature (usually) only visible to her. To hide the bone, the Hider enlists the aid of his power animal as well. In a really lively game, a whole host of other invisible animals will also take part. And both teams will work hard to hinder their opponents.

Shamanism is the very earliest known form of magic on the planet. It dates back to... Actually, nobody knows how far it dates back. You can be sure there were shamans in the Old Stone Age. You can be reasonably sure there were shamans even earlier. There's a cave painting of a shaman in France that's more than 20,000 years old. There are shamans (known as *clever men*) among Australia's Aborigines. That's a culture believed to run back in an unbroken line for at least 75,000 years.

Shamanism has been practised in every corner of our world, from the frozen wastes of Siberia –

where the word *shaman* comes from – to the steaming jungles of the Amazon. Although there are some differences from place to place, almost all of it is based on the idea that there are three worlds – an Upper, Middle and Lower. A properly trained shaman can get into all of them.

For the Middle World this is no great trick. It's the one we live in now, the world of planes and buses, computers, school books, television and germs. But the other two are something else. They're *spirit* worlds.

To reach the spirit worlds, some shamans take mind-altering drugs – ayahuasca, mescal, peyote, fly agaric and many others – several of which are deadly if you get the dose wrong. But most shamans just *ride the drum*.

The brain inside your skull is an electrical machine. The electricity it generates takes on wave forms that depend on your state of mind. Awake and excited you create one sort of brainwave. Fast asleep you produce another. You can change your brainwaves by relaxing deeply or sharply focusing your concentration. You can also change them with a drum.

Nobody quite knows why, but the human brain has a tendency to match waveforms with any strong rhythm in its vicinity. It could be a flashing light, or a tapping foot, or a drumbeat.

The process is known as *entrainment*. It explains why strobe lights can trigger epileptic fits and headbangers bang their heads at pop concerts. The raw two/four beat of rock-and-roll entrained teenagers so violently when it was first unleashed that they ran about breaking windows and smashing cinema seats.

A different rhythm sends you into trance. In that trance, if you know how, you can visit spirit worlds.

For most shamans, their first spirit visit is to the Lower World. Shamanic power largely depends on finding and befriending a power animal. The Lower World is where it lives.

Reaching the Lower World isn't all that difficult – I've taught the method to scores of people and not one failed to make the trip. If you want to follow suit, you'll need to know what shamanic drumming sounds like. In the old days, this meant a trip down the Amazon or a trek across Siberia. Now you can buy a CD from the Foundation for Shamanic Studies, set up by an American professor named Michael Harner.*

You can use the CD directly and it will work just fine. Alternatively, you can buy a shamanic drum and have a friend play it for you when you take your trip.

* You can reach the foundation at www.shamanism.org.

But that's getting a little ahead of the game. Before you go in search of the Lower World, you need to find your entrance. Take yourself off and look for it. What you're looking for is an opening into the ground. This might be a hole at the base of a tree, the entrance to an underground cave, maybe the burrow of an animal like a rabbit or a fox.

When you find it – some people tell me theirs 'called to them' – *memorise what it looks like*. Make a drawing if this helps or take a photograph. The point is that before you can reach the Lower World, you *must* be able to visualise your entrance clearly in your mind.

(Don't be tempted just to make it up. Trust me, that won't work. The entrance inside your head must have its counterpart in the physical world.)

Once you've memorised your entrance, you're ready for your trip. Find somewhere you won't be disturbed. Set up your drumming CD or instruct a friend to drum the basic shamanic rhythm. This should go on *for no more than twenty minutes*. After that he drums the recall.

The recall is a special rhythm that lets you, the journeying shaman, know it's time to come home. It's faster and louder than the basic rhythm and your friend should continue to drum it for at least a minute. You don't have to worry about any of this if you're using a journey-work CD, which will have everything already recorded.

Now make yourself comfortable. Sit or lie down. If it's cold, cover yourself with a blanket –

you tend to lose body heat while journeying. Relax completely and close your eyes when the drumbeat starts.

For the first few minutes, simply listen to the drum. Let the beat relax you further and carry you away inside your head. This is the process known as *riding the drum*. Then, in your own time, visualise your entrance.

It may be that the entrance in the physical world you discovered was too small for you to walk into – a rabbit hole, for example. But that won't stop you now. You can either enlarge the opening in your mind's eye until it's big enough to walk through or, alternatively, shrink yourself until you're small enough to fit.

Now walk in.

Inside your entrance you may find a tunnel or a cave or a whole series of caves. But if you explore carefully you'll finally discover a passageway leading downwards. Follow it, negotiating any obstacles you come across, until you see a light ahead. Make for that light and in a moment you'll emerge into the Lower World.

What the Lower World looks like varies from person to person. You're dealing with non-ordinary reality here and you mustn't expect it to behave the way your familiar world does.

Besides which, the Lower World is a big

place. The point where you enter it could be a long way from where others began their explorations.*

Take time to look around and find your feet. Get a feel for where you are and study the various landmarks.

Don't be in a hurry to find your power animal. It *may* turn up on your first trip, but some shamans have had to journey repeatedly before they got lucky. The reality is you don't find your power animal – it finds *you*. At some stage of your journey-work you'll come across animal beings. Steer clear of reptiles and insects – they're tricky – but if you find a friendly mammal or bird, feel free to ask, 'Are you my power animal?' If it is, it will  tell you so; and henceforth act as your guide.

While all this is going on, you're still riding the drum. When you hear the recall, you should immediately begin to retrace your steps in the Lower World, returning the way you came until

---

* Somebody mentioned to me the other day that there's a project afoot to map the entire Lower World by comparing reports from shamanic practitioners. It's an interesting idea, but so far I haven't been able to track down any further details.

you find your entrance tunnel and emerge back into the Middle World by opening your eyes.

Don't bring anything back with you. This is a magical adventure, not a holiday. It's no place for souvenirs. Your power animal will often accompany you to the Lower World side of your entrance, but after that you're on your own. You should come back with nothing more than you had with you when you went in.

Your power animal is not your servant, so mind your manners and treat it well. If you don't, it will walk and your shamanic career stops there. If you do, it will feed you energy and confidence and help you face problems in the physical world.

But the relationship is a two-way street. The deal is that you should dance your power animal at least once a month. Dancing your animal involves creating an impromptu dance in which you move as your power animal moves – the shambling Bear, the stalking Puma, etc. – for ten or fifteen minutes.*

While you dance, allow yourself to 'become' your power animal so it sees through your eyes. The theory is that dancing your animal allows it to experience the Middle World.

* Like so much magical work, you'd be advised to do this privately, otherwise people will think you're nuts.

Dancing isn't the only way to do this. Here we're right back where we started, with Find the Bone. If you're the Seer in this game, you call up your power animal and send it to find the bone, watching with your mind's eye which hand it sniffs out.

Members of the Seer's team strive quietly to create a mental Shield of Tranquillity that allows their Seer to concentrate. Members of the Hider team range their power animals defensively, then do everything they can to break the Seer's concentration. They're not allowed actually to say anything, but they can shout, dance, drum, shake rattles, make animal noises and sing mindless, non-vocal songs.

The power animals love it.

3
Wizard Training

In the old days – and even now in some parts of the world – it was no fun becoming a wizard. There were parts of Africa where you had to have epilepsy. There were parts of Australia where they shoved bits of rock crystal underneath your skin and left them to fester. There were parts of the Amazon where you had to drink plant brews so toxic it was touch and go whether you survived. There were ordeals that sent you mad, ordeals that left you crippled, ordeals that froze you, ordeals that burned you, ordeals that nearly drowned you. There were even ordeals where bits of you were eaten.

Wizardry is easier today. But not a lot.

Serious magical training has one very tricky side effect. It stirs up your unconscious.

By the time you're thirteen – and sometimes sooner – most of you have things in your unconscious that you'd rather leave alone.

Nasty shocks, painful memories, shameful fantasies, overwhelming fears… all the stuff that comes with life. You cope with it by forgetting it. You bury it down deep. You lock it up securely in the darkest corners of your mind and throw away the key.

Magical training lets it out again. That can be hard to take. It's one reason why wise wizards say you should get to know yourself before you start. Unfortunately, that means costly therapy or even psychoanalysis, which probably explains why so few wizards ever bother. As a result, emotional problems are common in the magical community.

On the face of it, you'd wonder why. Almost the whole of magical training involves just two harmless practices – meditation and visualisation.

There are various types of meditation, some easy, some hard. But the starting point of magical meditation is very simple. You're given a subject and told to think about it for ten minutes.

The *way* you're supposed to think about it is simple, too.

First, find yourself a spot where you won't be disturbed. Turn off your mobile phone. Sit in a comfortable upright chair. Upright is important.

If you use an easy chair or lie down on a bed, there's a risk you'll doze off. In an upright chair, dozing off leads to falling off, which wakes you up. Wizards are nothing if not practical.

Now start to relax.

Most people think they're relaxed when they're not. To deal with this, your first meditations should start with something called *progressive relaxation*. Begin with your feet. Curl your toes downwards to tighten them up *and notice what the tension feels like*. That's important. It lets you recognise tension when you see it. When you've noted the tension, let it go. That lets you recognise relaxation.

Now move up to your calf muscles, tighten and let go. Think about the difference between the tension and the relaxation. Then do your knees, then your thighs and so on until you've reached the very top of your head. (You can tighten your scalp muscles by frowning.)

By the time you're finished – and it only takes a few minutes when you get the hang of it – you'll know what tension feels like, you'll know what letting go of tension feels like and, most importantly, you'll find yourself very relaxed.

You can continue using progressive relaxation as long as you like – I still use it after forty years

– but a lot of trainee wizards move on to breathing exercises, which help relaxation and have other benefits as well. This is a beginner's book and I don't want to get complicated, but you might like to try the basic technique of *following your breath.*

Sit in your comfortable upright chair, close your eyes and think about your breathing. That's it. You don't have to control your breath or hold your breath or even deepen your breath. You just have to watch it. Let your mind follow your breath all the way in and all the way out. Doesn't sound much, but it's surprisingly relaxing.

Now you've relaxed, start to meditate on your chosen subject. Except that if you're training to be a wizard, it'll be your *given* subject. The school you're with, or the master wizard you're apprenticed to will pick something suitable for you to think about. One subject I saw handed down recently was 'The boundless sea of energy in which we live and breath and have our being'.

Lots of scope there. You take the boundless energy sea as your starting point and follow the subject through for ten minutes. At this point your alarm clock goes off and you stop. At least that's the theory. In practice, after thirty seconds or so you'll find you're not thinking about the boundless sea at all – you're thinking about luuurve or wondering if you fed the cat.

As part of your training, you have to make a note each time this happens. No big deal. No beating yourself up. Just a note under one of three headings: *Mind Wandering, Noises* and *Breaks*. The first heading is for those feed-the-cat moments. The second is when the sound of a plane crash outside distracts you. The third is for everything else.

At the end you write down any realisations you reached about the energy sea.

The mind-wandering notes are more important than the realisations. Your teachers will never admit it, but they don't give a toss what realisations you had.* That's just *theory*. That's just *speculation*. The practical purpose of wizard meditation is to train your powers of concentration. Making notes of the breaks will allow you to look back in a few months' time and see how you're doing.

After a while the breaks become fewer and fewer as you develop your powers. They'll continue to get fewer even after you increase your meditation time. (Up to a maximum of twenty minutes for a beginner.)

* Well, only a very little toss.

Eventually you'll find you can lock in like a laser. You wouldn't be distracted if you had to meditate in Piccadilly Circus.

Later on, trainee wizards learn another sort of meditation. For this you relax as before, but there's no subject for you to think about. Instead, you stop thinking altogether. Try this:

Close your eyes and begin to count at the rate of one a second. Think of nothing except the number you've reached. The second you discover you *are* thinking of something else – *'Hey, I'm counting really well!'* – you should stop. Chances are you won't have reached ten. And that's not even thinking of nothing, which is harder than thinking of counting. But with practice, wizards get the hang of it and can hold their minds completely blank for minutes at a time.

Meditation is only half the battle, however, and not even the biggest half.* In wizardry, the rest is visualisation.

Chances are you've done visualisation all your life. When you daydream. When you imagine how you're going to spend your second million. When you think about your perfect date.

Wizard visualisation isn't just *seeing* things with your mind's eye. It's *hearing* them with the

* Halves can be very odd in magic.

mind's ear, *touching* them, *tasting* them, *smelling* them as well. And doing it so vividly that you could, if necessary, count the leaves on an imagined bush... and feel the texture of each one.

The secret, once again, is practice. A good place to start is *Kim's Game*, first described by Rudyard Kipling in his children's novel *Kim*.

To play the game get somebody to lay out between twelve and twenty small objects on a tray and cover them with a cloth. When you're ready, remove the cloth and stare at the objects for exactly one minute. Then cover them up again and write down as many as you can remember, *along with its position on the tray*.

Kim's Game is a workout for your visual memory. In wizard training you'll be given further exercises to strengthen all your other inner senses. These vary from school to school, but one you might enjoy has to be done with a friend.

Lie down on the floor and have your friend lie down beside you so your heads are side by side, but your feet are pointing in opposite directions. Both of you should close your eyes. Now take this starting point for a story:

We are standing together at a lonely crossroads somewhere in the middle of a strange country. To the north, on the horizon, we can see the ruins of an ancient

31

castle. To the south lies a small town. The road eastwards is part concealed by mist. The road westwards disappears into a forest.

Decide between you which road you're going to take. Then build yourselves an adventure by describing, turn and turn about, what you see, what you hear and what happens. Don't let the session run for more than twenty minutes, however much fun it turns out to be.

(It hasn't reached the wizard schools yet, but I discovered some years ago that role play games like *Dungeons and Dragons* are great training for the magical imagination. The only drawback is you need groups of half a dozen or more to play them properly. Role play games on a computer – even multi-player versions – don't really hack it, since the pictures are on the screen and not inside your head.)

At a more advanced level, wizards work towards something called *interiorising* objects. Basically, you look at an object then allow what you're seeing physically to slide smoothly into your inner eye. This means you are, in effect, seeing the object as you would in a dream... but staying awake.

The first time I managed it was while reading a book. In that weird moment, I discovered it was actually possible to continue reading with my eyes closed.

The process works with sounds as well.

Sit with your eyes shut while a friend reads to you from a familiar book.* Have her stop at a particular point while you try to transfer her spoken words to your inner ear. If you manage it, you'll hear her as if she was still speaking.

At a more advanced level still, wizards learn to reverse the process. They make, let's say, a mental picture of a rose, then try to project it

* One of mine would be ideal.

outwards so that they see it as if it were physically present between their cupped hands. In effect they're creating a controlled hallucination.

There's a persistent rumour abroad that *some* wizards can project the rose so powerfully others can see it as well as themselves. But that's far too eerie to examine so early in the book.

4

Magic Afoot

If you decide to try any of the mind-training exercises mentioned in the last chapter, you'll discover two strange things.

The first is that your mind really doesn't want to be trained. In fact, it so doesn't want to be trained that it'll play tricks to make you stop. These can range from persuading you to forget the training session all the way to giving you a headache and making you feel tired or ill. One wizard I know got panic attacks.

Your mind is cunning. It figures (usually quite rightly) that physical symptoms will scare you enough to make you stop the training. Your mind is a creature of habit. It has its own ways of thinking and doesn't want to change them. But the problem is also the solution. If you ignore the symptoms and keep at it, there comes a day when your mind accepts the new patterns. At this point it will start fighting to maintain *them*.

Which brings me to the second strange thing. Even when your mind has settled comfortably into the training, you'll notice there are some times when results come easily and others when everything goes wrong.

You might imagine you've just had off-days. Wizards have a different theory. They believe there are unseen tides in the universe that work on your (unconscious) mind by way of the Earth's magnetic field. They also believe that if you note the position of the planets and the moon when your off-days occur, you can use the data to predict when things are likely to go right.*

The idea of unseen tides is hard to swallow, but consider the following:

In 1805, while the French author Emile Deschamps was still a boy at boarding school, he and several other pupils were invited to dinner with a man named de Fontgibu. The dessert was plum pudding. That's a rarity in France and Deschamps had never tasted it before. He took to it immediately.

From then on, Deschamps kept an eye out for his favourite dessert. Ten years later, he was dining in a restaurant near the Paris Opéra when he spotted plum pudding on the menu. He

---

* This personal experiment seems to be the real wizardry behind astrology, although many wizards firmly believe in traditional astrology as well.

ordered a portion, but an apologetic waiter told him the very last piece was just being served to a man at the next table. Deschamps turned to find the man was Monsieur de Fontgibu.

Years went by before Deschamps came across plum pudding again. In 1832 while attending a formal dinner, he discovered it was to be served for dessert. Deschamps remembered the coincidence in Paris and remarked to the hostess that the only thing needed to make the evening complete would be an appearance by M. de Fontgibu.

At that point, a very confused old man burst into the room. It was de Fontgibu. He'd been on

his way to another social gathering, but got lost. Then he mistook the house and gatecrashed Deschamps's dinner party.

This sort of thing happens more often than you'd think. In 1975, for instance, a man was killed by a taxi while riding his moped in Bermuda. A year later his brother was killed while riding the same moped. He was struck in the same street, by the same taxi, driven by the same driver and carrying the same passenger.

You can check the facts for yourself. A good place to start might be the parallels between the two American presidents, Abraham Lincoln and John F. Kennedy. These have been widely noted by journalists and historians, but never satisfactorily explained.

Lincoln was elected to Congress in 1846. Kennedy was elected to Congress in 1946. Lincoln was elected President in 1860. Kennedy was elected President in 1960. Both their names contain seven letters. Both became associated with Civil Rights. Both had wives who lost children while in the White House.

Lincoln's secretary was named Kennedy. Kennedy's secretary was called Lincoln. Both men were shot in the head on a Friday. John Wilkes Booth, who assassinated Lincoln, ran from a theatre and was caught in a warehouse.

Lee Harvey Oswald, who assassinated Kennedy, ran from a warehouse and was caught in a theatre. Both were themselves assassinated before they could be brought to trial. Both had fifteen letters in their names. Booth was born in 1839. Oswald was born in 1939.

The two Presidents were each succeeded by Southerners named Johnson. Andrew Johnson, who succeeded Lincoln, was born in 1808. Lyndon B. Johnson, who succeeded Kennedy, was born in 1908.*

All this is a matter of public record. You can check the details in your local library.

It's almost impossible to read stories like these without a nagging feeling that something's going on. You get the same feeling when you learn that twenty people are killed by dogs in the United States each year. That statistic hasn't varied by more than one or two for decades. It's the stability of the figure that's mysterious. How do the dogs know when to stop killing people?

At the same time, it's very difficult to figure out exactly what is happening. Most of our scientists are no help at all. They say it's just coincidence.

* Within two paragraphs of writing these words, I received a mass email from a fan who'd come across the same material and was busily distributing it across the Internet – an oddity in itself.

Unfortunately, the term *coincidence* is a description, not an explanation. It means, according to the *Oxford English Dictionary*:

a) occurring or being together.

b) an instance of this.

So all it really tells us is what we already knew: odd things happen at the same time. It doesn't tell you why.

Coincidence and Probability

Some coincidences can be explained mathematically, using probability theory. There's no doubt that this method – which uses maths to find out what the chances are of something happening – can throw up some surprises. For example, you only need 23 people in a room for a better than 50/50 chance that two of them have the same birthday. Pack in another 77 and the chances hit more than *3 million* to one.*

Fortunately, some scientists weren't happy with the dismissive description. One of them was the Austrian biologist Paul Kammerer. Kammerer was fascinated by coincidence. At age

* 3,254,690 to one, to be exact.

twenty, he started to keep a log of everyone he heard about or experienced. He recorded them faithfully for the next twenty years.

Most were trivial. Once his brother-in-law went to a concert where his seat number (9) turned out to be the same as his cloakroom ticket number. The following night he went to another concert where his seat number (21) was the same as his cloakroom ticket number.

Some were more complicated, but not very important, like this peculiar sequence of events:

Kammerer's wife was reading a novel about a character named Mrs Rohan. She caught a tram and on it saw a man who looked strikingly like her friend Prince Josef Rohan. Somebody asked this man whether he knew the village of Weissenbach on Lake Attersee. Mrs Kammerer got off the tram and went into a shop where the assistant promptly asked her if she happened to know the village of Weissenbach on Lake Attersee. That evening, Prince Rohan came calling.

Eventually Kammerer became so intrigued that he took to spending hours on park benches making notes about the people who walked past. In theory they should have wandered by at random, but they didn't. He noticed that they tended to clump together according to particular characteristics. If you saw a man carrying a parcel, you could be sure one or two other parcel-carriers would turn up soon after. This seems similar to a mechanism long noted by the medical profession. One professor is on record as remarking to his students, 'Gentlemen, today we examine a case that is absolutely unique in the annals of medicine. Within a week, we shall have three more just like it.' It is as if like somehow attracts like.

All this led Kammerer to the conclusion that there was some sort of hidden connection between certain events that had nothing to do with cause and effect. (Carrying your parcel past a park bench didn't *cause* other people to do the same, but there was still a connection.) Kammerer, who published a book on his theory, didn't try to say what the connection actually was, but two other distinguished scientists – the physicist Wolfgang Pauli and the psychologist Carl Jung – thought the link might be the human mind.

Wizards came to exactly the same conclusion centuries ago. The idea that like attracts like is one of the oldest magical principles in the world. African tribal rainmakers sprinkle water on the parched ground to 'call' rain* – a process known

* At least that's the part of the process everybody can see. There's actually a bit more to it than that.

as sympathetic magic. It doesn't work every time, but it works often enough to make it worthwhile. And it works best when carried out by a trained wizard – that's to say, someone who has disciplined his or her mind.

In modern magical practice, wizards use the hidden connections between events as indicators that their magic is effective. The process is known as an *Earth Plane Check*.

The Earth Plane Check is particularly important when you're engaged in magic that's not designed to produce tangible results. One wizard friend of mine took it into her head that she'd like to chat with the Greek god Apollo in the hope of getting his help on some research work she was doing.

She created a ritual based on some very old Greek religious ceremonies, prepared her place of working, lit her incense and called on the god. It seemed as if the operation worked. In her mind's eye – which is where most magical work takes place – she 'saw' the golden figure arise and 'heard' the advice he gave her.

But wizards are neither stupid nor naïve. She realised the results she'd achieved could easily be wishful thinking or simply her own imagination. So she asked for an Earth Plane Check.

That afternoon she went shopping. (Something

wizards do just like everybody else.) As she entered the mall, her eye was caught by a massive plastic sun, part of an advertising promotion for sunscreen lotion. She was alerted at once – Apollo is a sun-god – but knew better than to pay too much attention to a single sign.

As she walked past the travel agent, however, she discovered a brand-new window display calling on customers to… BOOK YOUR HOLIDAY IN GREECE, LAND OF ETERNAL SUNSHINE. A photograph of an appealing Greek island was overshadowed by an artist's impression of the sun-god himself. Beside the agency, a jeweller's shop announced a special 'Gold Week' – the metal closely associated with Apollo.

My friend was heartened by the developments, but her Earth Plane Check wasn't finished yet. Before returning home, she passed a teenage couple wearing matching T-shirts, each featuring the single word APOLLO. Outside the mall she found parked a bus emblazoned with the name APOLLO TOURS along its side.

Her final call of the day was to her favourite bookshop. She was reaching for a book on astrology when she accidentally knocked a bulky paperback off a nearby shelf. The title was *Failure is Not an Option* by someone called Gene Kranz. She picked it up and was putting it back on the shelf when she noticed the subtitle: *Mission Control from Mercury to Apollo 13.*

At which point she decided her contact with the sun-god had been genuine.

5
So You'd Like to Be a Wizard?

There's a saying in Haiti: *What you see... it's not what you think.* Wizardry is just the opposite: *What you think... it's not what you see.*

The trouble is, what you think seems to be what you learned from fairy tales. When somebody tells you magic really exists, your mind goes to Christmas pantos, Disney movies and Harry Potter stories. Suddenly your head's full of witches flying on broomsticks, Sleeping Beauty's enchantment, Cinderella's Fairy Godmother. You want to see an invisibility cloak. Or watch a portrait come to life.

(Or maybe you start worrying about the darker magic that somehow seems more likely than the fairy tales: the ghosts, the zombies, the vampires, Mephistopheles appearing in a puff of smoke, complete with horns and scarlet cloak.)

It doesn't work like that. If you ever watch

David Copperfield change a pumpkin into a coach with the wave of a wand, you can be quite sure it's a trick. But at the same time, a lot of the old fairy stories and much of folklore is based on actual magic. It's often exaggerated, sometimes distorted, but the roots are real.

People who want to be wizards need to know what they're getting into *before* they take the training. Which is not as easy as it sounds. Many wizards won't talk about what they do. And those who will talk often exaggerate to make themselves look important. So for the rest of this chapter, I propose to fill you in on the reality behind some of the stories – without exaggeration or unnecessary secrecy.

BURIED TREASURE

The Legend

This is a branch of wizardry you don't hear much about now, but it used to be huge up to the end of the seventeenth century.

In those days there was no real banking system. People kept spare cash and precious objects safe by hiding them. Often this involved literally taking a spade, digging a hole and burying the lot. Despite the romantic stories, very few drew up treasure maps – there was too great a chance of them falling into the wrong hands. If you buried treasure, the best thing to do was keep the location in your head.

The trouble was you could forget where you buried it. Or, more often, die without telling anybody. As a result, the countryside was littered with buried treasure* and wizards were among those who went berserk trying to get their hands on it.

A typical case involved a young English aristocrat named Goodwin Wharton (1653–1704). Although he came from a wealthy family, he managed to go through money like a sailor on a Saturday night. As a result he was broke by his early twenties. His father bailed him out a few times, but then lost patience and left Goodwin to his own devices.

Goodwin was ill-qualified to earn a living[†] and decided his future lay in finding buried treasure. Like most people of his time, he believed the best way to do this was to use magic. Since it was too much bother to learn it himself, he contacted a professional wizard named Mary Parish.

Unfortunately, Mary wasn't much of a wizard.

* Or so people believed.
† So useless, in fact, that the only job he ever got was as a Member of Parliament – and that only came up in later life.

48

In fact, the term *con artist* springs to mind. She claimed to be able to talk to angels and some very high-ranking fairies, all of whom were happy to pinpoint treasure locations. But when Mary and Goodwin went looking, something always stopped them finding the gold.

Mostly it was Guardian Spirits. According to the current theory, nearly all treasure was protected by spirits who had to be placated before you could dig it up. Often they had to be bribed. Goodwin would borrow money and hand it over to Mary who would pass it on to the spirits. But always the spirits would welsh on the deal. Sometimes they moved the treasure to another spot. Sometimes they placed impossible conditions on Goodwin before he was allowed to dig.

Goodwin funded more unsuccessful treasure hunts than you'd think possible for a man who could buckle his own shoes. But then again, he also believed Mary when she said she had miraculously borne a child of his* and that the Queen of the Fairies wanted to marry him.

The story of Goodwin Wharton is an extraordinary example of what can happen if

* He never saw the offspring, but contributed to its upkeep.

you buy into too much nonsense about wizardry. The world is still full of con artists like Mary Parish, all claiming magical powers and selling fairy tales to those fool enough to listen.

But is there any real truth in the rumour that wizards can locate buried treasure?

The Reality

Surprisingly, the answer is yes. There really is a magical technique that will allow you to locate things buried in the ground, including gold and gems. But it has nothing to do with talking to angels or outwitting spirit guardians. What Goodwin Wharton should have done was find himself a wizard skilled in *dowsing*.

In Goodwin's day, dowsing was known as *water witching* and seen as one of the magical arts. Today, dowsing for water is widely accepted, although scientists insist there's nothing magical about it. But that's dowsing in the field with a forked stick. There's another way of dowsing, which I'll teach you later in this book, that is absolutely magical in nature.

The wizard who went public about it was the late Tom C. Lethbridge, who wasn't known as a wizard in his lifetime, but as an archaeologist. During a long, distinguished career, he built up a reputation for finding hitherto undiscovered megalithic sites. He let his scientific colleagues assume it was experience and skill that guided him. But after he retired, he admitted the truth. Many of his major finds were the result of map dowsing. He'd kept the technique a secret because he thought his professional standing would suffer if anybody found out.

Magic is more an art than a science. You can learn it the way you might learn to play the piano – how well you work it will depend partly on practice, partly on natural talent. That said, map dowsing is one of the easier wizard arts, so there's a very good chance you'll get results when you come to try it.

But don't expect too much in the way of buried treasure. Most people keep their valuables in banks these days, so there's not a lot of it about.*

CONJURATION

The Legend

It's as scary as it gets. In the small hours of the morning, the black-robed wizard creeps into the empty basement. By the flickering light of a tallow candle, he draws a magic circle on the

---

* Not to mention the fact that, in many countries, the Government lays claim to much or all of what you find.

stone-flagged floor. To the north of the circle he inscribes an equilateral triangle. He lights incense, opens up an ancient tome. In a resonant, sepulchral voice, he begins to read an eldritch conjuration.

You've stumbled on a scene in horror books and fantasies. (I must confess I have a liking for it in my own fiction.) You've seen it in the movies, on TV. You know exactly what will happen next.

A mist forms in the triangle. Something evil this way comes. There is a pervasive smell of sulphur. The mist solidifies into a shape. Two fiery eyes glare out into the room. Gradually the thing inside the triangle takes on solid form. It has horns, claws and a scaly skin. And yet its shape is vaguely human...

The legend of the conjuration is as old as magic itself. From the earliest of shamanic times, every wizard worth his salt has been attributed the ability to conjure (call up) and command spirits, although the circle/triangle technique I described above only dates back to the Middle Ages.

Some wizards, like Queen Elizabeth I's Court Astrologer Dr John Dee, called up angels. Others, like the notorious Dr Faustus – who was alive and well in Germany during the late sixteenth century – made a pact with the Devil.

Stories of conjuration reached a worldwide audience, not least due to William Shakespeare who introduced spirits into several of his plays. *The Tempest*, for example, is full of them. The drama's central character, Prospero, is, of course, a wizard. But in *Henry IV, Part 1*, Shakespeare put a cynical little exchange in the mouths of two of his characters:

GLENDOWER   *I can call spirits from the vasty deep.*

HOTSPUR   *Why, so can I, or so can any man; But will they come when you do call for them?*

Well, will they?

The Reality

Conjuration is probably the trickiest and most dangerous of all magical operations. (Which is why you won't find out how to do it from this book.) If it's done well, the answer to Hotspur's question is yes, the spirits will come. But what you think is not what you'll (probably) see.

To understand a conjuration, you have to go back to the shamanic roots of magic. When a shaman wants to make contact with the spirit world, he goes into a trance state. In this state he can see spirits and talk to them. But those around him can't.

When clever – and smug – Western scientists began to study shamanism in the twentieth century, they took this to mean the 'spirits' weren't real. They existed only in the shaman's imagination. He made them up the way Dickens made up Mr Pickwick.

From the start, there were a few problems with this theory. First of all, peculiar things sometimes happened when the shaman talked to spirits. Among the native North Americans, for example, the tent might begin to shake violently. Or in Haiti, a spirit talking to the shaman might jump into one of the spectators and take him over for a while.

But since facts should never get in the way of a good theory, most of the scientists stuck to their guns.* As a result, you'll still hear it claimed that spirits are 'all imagination'.

Oddly enough, wizards agree. But they part company with the scientists in their ideas about the nature of imagination.

In scientific circles, imagination is just the ability of your mind to make moving pictures inside your head. When you go to sleep, it helps

---

* But to be fair, not all. A few of the more open-minded scientists began to suspect there was more going on than met the eye.

you dream. If it's out of control, you get sick and hallucinate. There's nothing more to it than that.

But to a wizard, imagination is evidence of the divine.* It's a gateway to the spirit worlds – and one that works both ways. Of course you can use it to mock up your own pictures. But intelligent entities from beyond our reality can use it too. Given encouragement, they can set up powerful lines of communication directly into your brain. Indeed, they sometimes walk right in there, sit down and take over. You can see why conjuration is so dangerous. You're unlocking a door to your mind and inviting aliens to come on in and party.

So conjuration is a purely *mental* phenomenon? Well… not quite. It *can* all take place inside your head – and an experienced wizard will work hard to make sure it stays there – but there are persistent rumours about conjurations to *visible appearance*. Students in the Golden Dawn were expected to call up spirits that were visible at least to the degree of a fine mist.

I don't know whether conjuration to visible appearance is still done today. I've never seen it. But most modern conjurations aren't quite confined to the head either. Typically, the first

* A phrase coined by the great London poet, painter and visionary William Blake.

sign of success is a change of atmosphere inside the room. There's often a drop in temperature, as if the spirits were sucking out energy. And if you can't actually see anything inside the triangle, you can certainly sense a presence. It's not always pleasant.

Sometimes, if you're particularly unlucky, things can happen that make a shaking tent look feeble. Several years ago, I was involved with a group of some thirty wizards in a conjuration experiment that used the circle/triangle technique. Three of the wizards were stationed at the triangle corners.

At the moment the spirit was called, one of them – a hefty six-foot-four Bishop of the Liberal Catholic Church – was lifted eighteen inches into the air and flung back against a wall. He slid back down slowly, gasping and choking.

CURSES

The Legend

It's long been believed there are people who can lay curses that will leave people barren, luckless, ill or even dead. Sometimes the belief was light-hearted, like the superstition that a gypsy could curse you by turning his cap backwards. Sometimes it was deadly serious. Scores of witches – or supposed witches – were burned at the stake after accusations they had cursed their neighbours.

The intensity of the witch-hunts, which stretched from the fourteenth to the eighteenth centuries, shows how seriously people took the whole idea of curses. There are still parts of the world today – by no means primitive either – where a careless hand gesture or even a peculiar look can get you accused of laying a curse.

But is such a thing actually possible?

The Reality

Aboriginal clever men in parts of Australia will sometimes use the *pointing bone* against those who've seriously wronged them. The bone, decorated in a shamanic rite, is pointed at the victim who then sickens and dies.

There have been several scientific studies of the pointing bone in Australia and similar forms of curse elsewhere in the world. In the more extreme cases, even Western medical intervention failed to save the victim's life.

The scientists concluded that the mechanism of the curse was suggestion. The simple tribesman was brought up from birth to believe in the power of the witch-doctor. When he saw the pointing bone, he decided he was doomed and literally willed himself to death. The scientists speculated that if you didn't believe in the first place, you'd be immune to the curse.

I've no doubt suggestion does play a part. But it doesn't seem to be the whole story. I've personally experienced two effective curses that were laid without my knowledge. I picked up the first from handling a Tibetan ritual knife. The thing felt unpleasant and within an hour I was plunged into an irrational depression that lasted until I realised what was happening and took (wizard) steps to break the influence.

Dealing with the second was a lot less easy. I found myself stricken with a skin rash that defied all medical treatment. After several months, a therapist suggested the root cause might be a curse. I investigated, came to the conclusion she was right and took magical countermeasures. Interestingly, these didn't clear the rash directly. But the various creams that had failed so miserably for several months suddenly became effective and banished it overnight.

The methods of laying a curse on a person are not taught in any of the reputable magical schools. But they are, unfortunately, fairly easy to work out once you've reached a certain stage of your training.

I'm not sure that laying a curse against property is really possible – if it is, it's certainly not easy – but unscrupulous wizards can *simulate* a property curse by letting you know about it. This time it really *is* suggestion. Accidents happen to everyone, but if you think you've been cursed and your house happens to burn down, you'll give credit to the wizard.

ENCHANTMENT

The Legend
The *Oxford English Dictionary* defines the term *enchant* as 'charm... delight... bewitch'. Folklore abounds with stories of villains, male and female, who did just that to the heroes of the stories. It happened to the Wizard Merlin, no mean enchanter himself. He ended his life bewitched, befuddled and magically locked up in a crystal cave.

The Reality

Enchantment is still commonplace today, except it isn't called enchantment any more. It usually involves a mixture of charisma, hypnosis, celebrity, sex appeal and psychological manipulation – wizard arts that have now leaked out into the general community.

In modern times, the best example of mass enchantment was Hitler's power over the German people. Historians have tried to explain his extraordinary influence in political, social and economic terms. Wizards know better.

A few years before the First World War, Hitler (then in his early twenties with ambitions to become a painter) spent some time bumming around Vienna. He was interested in subjects like hypnosis, astrology and mind-power, so his wanderings took him into second-hand book shops. One of them was owned by a man named Ernst Pretsche.

Pretsche looked like a horror baddie out of Central Casting. He was a short, fat toad of a man with warts and a hunchback. He was also a black magician. He took an immediate interest in the young Hitler.

At first their conversations were confined to books, but Pretsche eventually broached the subject of magic. He offered to teach Hitler the essentials of mind-control, then initiate him into the deeper mysteries of the esoteric arts. Hitler accepted at once.

After a period of study, Pretsche concluded his new apprentice was ready for initiation. He told Hitler to prepare himself. Hitler can scarcely have realised what he was getting into.

Pretsche was skilled in a magical system based on the heroic myths of King Arthur and his Knights of the Round Table – a system still in use in several wizardry schools today.* But there was something else in his background that made him doubly dangerous.

Pretsche's father, Johann Pretsche, was a botanist who spent much of his working life in Mexico. There he came across a little blue-green cactus used by Native American shamans in their magical and religious rituals. The cactus was peyote, a powerful hallucinogenic, unknown in Europe at the time. When he retired, Johann brought dried samples of the cactus back to Germany. On his death, these passed to his son Ernst, who read his father's notes, realised the mind-blowing effect of eating peyote and promptly incorporated it into his magical practice.

Peyote formed part of the sacrament offered to

---

* Myths are often used in magical training because of their profound effect on the human mind.

Hitler during his ceremonial initiation. It hurled him into a wildly altered state of consciousness, guided by the toad-like Pretsche, his magical mentor. And there, hallucinating wildly, he took the first steps on a road that led to war, conquest, the ruin of his country and the horrors of Buchenwald and Belsen.

Hitler had become a dark wizard.

FLYING BROOMSTICKS

The Legend

Ah, flying broomsticks! They were practically the first thing Harry Potter learned about at Hogwarts, but the legend is far older than the works of J. K. Rowling. From the mid-fourteenth century onwards, there was a widespread popular belief – fostered by the Church, among others – in the existence of organised witchcraft.

Witches throughout the country were supposed to have grouped themselves in covens – secret cells of thirteen members, a blasphemous imitation of Christ and his Twelve Disciples. Six times a year, at the great solar festivals of solstices and equinoxes, plus May Eve and All Hallows Eve, they attended night gatherings called Sabbats. There they pledged allegiance to the Devil (who somehow managed to get around all the Sabbats in a single night) by kissing him under his tail then engaged in acts of child-murder and unbridled lust.

Sabbats were said to be held in inaccessible places like Brocken in Germany, the Bald Mountain, near Kiev in Russia, the Blocula in Sweden and the Département du Puy-de-Dôme in the French Auvergne. To reach them, so the Holy Inquisition assured us, these wicked women placed a phallic broomstick between their legs and rode it through the night skies to their distant destination.

The Reality
The reality was that witches did indeed exist (and still do) even if internationally organised witchcraft did not. Some were the pagan remnants of a Goddess worship that had been the religion of prehistoric Europe. Others were cunning men and wise women who studied herb lore, simple charms and spells in order to eke out a living as healers and midwives. All were persecuted viciously by the Christian Church.

In the deadly atmosphere of the times, it's not surprising that witches longed for the comfort and security of meeting with their peers. But there was no question of gathering physically. The world was far too dangerous for that. So they made use of something known as *flying ointment*.

The active ingredient in flying ointment was aconite (thorn-apple) a poisonous plant that triggered hallucinations if it didn't kill you. Rubbed into the skin, it found its way into the bloodstream through cuts or scratches. (*Everybody* in the Middle Ages had cuts and scratches.)

Thus, in a magical ceremony as effective as it was pitiable, followers of the ancient Craft removed their clothes to anoint their bodies with aconite ointment, straddled the traditional broomstick, then fell down in a faint for a few hours' release from their troubles as their minds flew away to their dream-like gatherings.

GHOSTS

The Legend
You know all the legends about ghosts. They haunt houses. They flit along the battlements of lonely castles. They walk through walls. They disappear when you least expect it.

But what have ghosts got to do with wizards?

The Reality
Wizards can *make* ghosts. The experiment was successfully carried out in England by a group of

wizards – mainly female – who came together specially for the purpose. After considerable discussion, they decided their artificial ghost would be based on a pre-Roman Saxon priestess called Coventina. The operation took five days and involved novel use of numerology and sacred geometry.

During a ritual climax, Coventina manifested by speaking through one of the group like a Spiritualist medium. The others questioned her for about twenty minutes. Then the experiment concluded in order to protect the medium, who was by then showing signs of stress.

Some years earlier, a Canadian group took several months to create a ghost named Philip, based on a purely fictional character who lived in Cromwellian England. This creation produced raps and poltergeist activity, including the levitation of a small table. Interestingly, 'Philip' was able to give the group information about life in the seventeenth century that was unknown to them at the time and formed no part of the original story.

According to at least one respected European source* Tibetan sorcerers have long been able to create artificial ghosts (which they call *tulpas*) by

* The distinguished French traveller Madame Alexandra David-Neel, who died in 1969 at the age of 101.

means of intense concentration and visualisation. The creatures can be seen by others.

INVISIBILITY

The Legend

One of the most popular stories about invisibility was written by H. G. Wells. His invisible man got the way he was by standing between two radiating centres of 'ethereal vibration', if I remember rightly. The weekly comics of my youth had great fun with the idea of children becoming invisible when they rubbed themselves with their mother's vanishing cream.

Many of the older invisibility legends are associated with magical cloaks. The stories typically tell of a traveller to a distant country – often the Holy Land, or elsewhere in the Middle East – who finds a concealed hoard that includes a mysterious cloak. He puts it on to ward off the evening chill and discovers that while he wears the cloak, nobody can see him.

The Reality

The Elizabethan magus, Dr John Dee, spent the best years of his life in a prolonged magical experiment designed to let him talk to angels. One result was the revelation of a whole new system of sorcery based on an angelic language known as Enochian. Part of the system was a technique for achieving invisibility based on the idea of surrounding yourself with a specially created *etheric egg* that stopped others seeing you.

I had the privilege of attempting an Enochian invisibility experiment with a group of ceremonial magicians in the Cotswolds some years ago. After hours of intense work, we were forced to admit failure. Our target, a courageous young man, remained stubbornly visible to everyone present.

A far more successful approach is invisibility through insignificance. This technique is based on the idea that if no one ever notices you, you are, for all practical purposes, invisible. Thus wizards practise holding themselves absolutely still in both body and mind in order to achieve insignificance.

Stilling the body is obvious. A static target is far more difficult to see than one that moves. This is something realised instinctively by prey animals, which often freeze when they sense a threat. Stilling the mind is based on a wizard belief that the mental racket we all make is picked up by others at an unconscious level. Thus halting the flow of thought while sitting still in an area outside the natural focus of a room, can lead to your being overlooked altogether. It's fun to try.

MAGIC MIRRORS

The Legend
'Mirror, mirror on the wall,
   Who is the fairest of them all?'
   The mirror assures the wicked queen that she is... until age begins to rob her of her looks and a young upstart is named in her place.

Lewis Carroll, who I suspect knew far more about wizardry than he let on, used a mirror as a plot device in his second most popular book, *Alice Through the Looking-Glass*. Mirrors are magic and always have been, even outside the magical community. Try this:

Stand in front of a full-length mirror and carefully draw around the reflection of your face with a marker or crayon. Now step back and look. The oval you've drawn is tiny compared with the reflection you were admiring a moment ago. The mirror has worked magic on you to shrink your head.

The Reality
For several centuries, the Chinese exported magical mirrors made from bronze with a

distinctive design on the back. When you held them up to the light, you could see right through to the embossed design. This was, of course, impossible and the mirrors remained a mystery until Western scientists eventually discovered the trick – and it *was* a trick – but only late in the twentieth century.

Mirrors are, however, extensively used in wizardry. Again in China (with no technical trickery involved) wizards deploy them to deflect bad influences or, using a different setting, to spread good luck.

In European wizardry, black mirrors often replace the traditional crystal ball in attempts to divine the future or see events at a distance. American wizards have now devised a technique which they claim allows them to conjure spirits into a concave mirror so they can be seen by others. In true American style they've issued a DVD of the operation.

Another wizardry technique uses an ordinary hand mirror and a lighted candle to show you your past lives. My wife, no mean wizard herself, was doing this when she fell into trance and set the plastic back of the mirror on fire. The roar of the flames awoke her and she found she was holding a flaring inferno. 'You deal with this,' she said, and handed it to me.

THE PHILOSOPHER'S STONE

The Legend

In the ancient practice of alchemy, the Philosopher's Stone was a much-sought-after substance. It was a powder or potion rather than an actual stone and it could be used to change base metals into gold. Later, alchemists took to claiming the 'stone' could also be used as a medicine for humans: it would cure all ills and prolong life indefinitely. For this reason the Stone was sometimes referred to as the Elixir of Immortality.

The Reality

Alchemy is now generally thought of as the primitive forerunner of modern chemistry. Modern chemistry, despite its sophistication, can't turn base metals into gold, although modern physics can.* So scientists assume our stupid ancestors couldn't possibly have managed the trick either.

There's no doubt that right back to the earliest practice of alchemy, there have been con artists who faked discovery of the Philosopher's Stone. You can get a nice gold-coloured substance by grinding down some metals and mixing them with sulphur. There are examples of alchemical gold in the British Museum that have been assayed as genuine. Science assumes they were switched by sleight of hand.

But the story of alchemy doesn't end there. The great psychologist Carl Jung suggested its tortuous processes weren't aimed at *literally* turning base metals into gold, but rather at refining the soul of the alchemist. The real aim was to turn him into a better person. The talk of turning a base metal into gold was purely symbolic.

Many modern wizards accept this theory. Some even practise what's called spiritual alchemy to get themselves in shape. A few go further. They claim that while Jung was right about the effect of alchemy on the mind, there's also a subtle connection between mind and

* But only in small quantities and at such an enormous cost it's not worth the bother.

matter. With enough training you can *really* turn lead into gold. This echoes claims by Taoist alchemists that certain Masters have disciplined themselves to achieve near-miraculous control of their bodies. As a result they are now immortal.

That said, I've yet to meet a 500-year-old alchemist with money to burn.

SPELLS

The Legend
Think of wizardry and you think of spells – special words or phrases spoken aloud to work magic. Most Harry Potter spells are one-worders, usually drawn from Latin, but the legend of the spell goes back thousands of years. There are spells on clay tablets that date to the first known civilisation. There are hieroglyphic spells painted on the walls of Egypt.

The Reality
I feel almost embarrassed to tell you there aren't very many spells in modern wizardry. They're a bit more common in witchcraft.

The closest I've come to spells in wizardry proper are the Calls of Enochian magic, a system I mentioned earlier. Dr Dee's angels took the precaution of dictating each Call letter-by-letter and backwards. The reason, they said, was that the words were so powerful they might stir up unwanted magical effects if pronounced aloud.

(I'm not sure the angels need have worried. The Calls contain strings of words like *DS ZONRENSG CAB ERM IADNAH*. Wizards have been arguing about their correct pronunciation for the last 400 years.)

The 'barbarous Words of Power' found in the older magical ceremonies are just as bad. Some are derived from the secret Names of God which, according to rabbinical tradition, should never be pronounced aloud. Others, I'm ashamed to say, seem to come from demons.

Despite the angels' claims, 'spells' of this type don't work automatically. If they work at all, it's by influencing the mind. The process is far clearer in the East where there's a type of spell – called a *mantra* – that's generally used in meditation, but has found its way into magic as well.

Mantras are often circular and can be repeated over and over like a snake swallowing its own tail. You can try this for yourself – it's quite safe. Use the Buddhist mantra *Om mani padme hum*. It translates as 'Hail to the jewel in the lotus' and refers to the spiritual essence of a human being.

Pronounce the mantra as AUMMM MA-

NEE PAD-MEY HUMMM. After you've said it aloud a few times, you'll notice how easily the *mmm* of the HUMMM blends into the AUMMM at the beginning, creating a circular mantra ideal for repetition.

Used mentally, a circular mantra 'throws off' extraneous thoughts like a spinning wheel. That's a huge aid to concentration – an important part of wizard training.

Witches' spells are a bit closer to the Harry Potter ideal. Usually the desired result of the spell is clear from the words chosen – *Thee I bless*, or whatever. But within the Craft, spells are frequently in rhyme, like this one designed to attract a lover, taught by my old witch friend Paddy Slade:

> *May my wish always be*
> *Right for you and right for me.*
> *May our love be strong and pure*
> *May it grow full and endure.*
> *Bring the one who's right for me*
> *That I may no longer be*
> *Alone and lonely in this plight*
> *Grant, I ask, this wish tonight.**

* If you're interested, you can find the full working of the spell – the rhyme is only part – in Paddy's superb book *Natural Magic*, Hamlyn, London, 1990.

It's not great poetry, but like most witch spells, it does have a driving rhythm. That greatly concentrates your mind on the task at hand. It's the mind that works the magic, not the words.

VAMPIRES

The Legend

My fellow countryman, Abraham Stoker, had a lot to answer for. He took a perfectly real – if very bloody – slice of history, mixed it with an ancient European myth and produced a book called *Dracula*, a name you will doubtless know well.

Christopher Lee has a lot to answer for as well. He played the role of Dracula so well he managed to make it sexy.

There was nothing sexy about the vampires of the original myth. They were just corpses, often middle-aged and pot-bellied, that refused to lie down. In some versions of the folklore, they sustained themselves by drinking blood and could only be laid to rest by decapitation or a stake through the heart.

The Dracula in Bram Stoker's book wasn't all that sexy either. He had a thick, drooping moustache and the smell of the grave about him. He did drink blood and avoided stakes though, unlike his historical role model, a warrior king called Vlad, who spilled blood and used stakes to impale his victims.

But behind all the flim-flam, the original legend remains. There's some sort of sorcery that allows dead bodies to climb out of their coffins and prey on the living.

But is the legend based on fact, or just the nightmare of children worried about their inheritance?

The Reality
One school of thought suggests the whole idea of vampirism started with anaemics in the Dark Ages. Anaemia is a blood disease that's easily treated today with iron injections. But left to run its course, it gives you a ferocious craving for the taste of blood. You can even find yourself fancying raw liver. Some academics reckon that in our distant past, the craving got out of control, a poor anaemic bit a passer-by in the neck and the whole vampire legend got started.

The drawback, of course, is that while anaemics may be sick, they're still very much alive until their condition kills them. And when it does, they're very much dead. There's no suggestion whatsoever that anaemia helps you rise from the grave.

I don't know many wizards who buy the anaemia theory. Most look on the vampire legends as a distortion of something they have to tackle occasionally as part of their wizard work – energy drains.

You've probably met one or two energy drains in your time. They're people who leave you utterly exhausted. They may be perfectly nice. They certainly aren't necessarily evil. They can even be quite entertaining. Yet there's something about them that sucks away your energy, leaving you washed out.

Wizards take energy drains very seriously and have devised protection techniques to block the loss. (There's a simple one given in the panel.) The link with undead mythology arises from the

---

Blocking a Drain

There are complicated rituals aimed at blocking an energy drain, but with practice you can do the job just as well with visualisation. Try this if you find yourself in the company of somebody who's exhausting you just by breathing:

Visualise yourself surrounded by a sphere of clear, clean blue-white light. Now imagine it spinning on an axis running from the top of your head to the soles of your feet.

The spinning sphere acts as a shield, keeping your own energy in while stopping interference from the outside. Obviously it's best for you to put the shield in place *before* you meet up with the troublesome person, but it will still work whenever you choose to use it.

---

fact that not all energy drains have physical bodies. Some manifest invisibly as ghosts or other entities, but remain quite capable of exhausting you in minutes.

WANDS

The Legend

When a wizard wants to cast a spell, he uses his wand – right? You've seen it a thousand times in the movies. You've read about it in books. There's usually a burst of light from the tip of the wand, often a trail of fairy dust, then the magic happens.

The Reality

Wizards really do use wands. Some are purely ceremonial, like the one on the right, which is a symbol of authority for an important official of a particular magical school.

Others are a bit more practical. The beautiful Lotus Wand (see next page) was a general-purpose wand used by members of the Golden Dawn. The coloured bands on the shaft equated with the Signs of the Zodiac and two alchemical symbols (shown on the left of the diagram). You gripped the wand by the band that ruled over the particular work.

It wasn't generally realised, even in the Golden Dawn itself, that the colours of this wand also reflected the energies that play along the human spine as they appear to psychical investigation. But here again is another indication that the implements of wizardry are designed to focus the mind rather than produce results in their own right.

✷	WHITE
♈	RED
♉	RED-ORANGE
♊	ORANGE
♋	AMBER
♌	YELLOW
♍	YELLOW-GREEN
♎	EMERALD
♏	GREEN-BLUE
♐	BLUE
♑	INDIGO
♒	VIOLET
♓	CRIMSON
▽	BLACK

The tradition of light flashing from the tip of a wand comes from the magical use of quartz crystal rods. Quartz has the curious property of turning one form of energy into another. If you go into a darkened room and tap one end of a quartz crystal (gently!) you will see a flash of light at the other. Kinetic energy (the tap) has been transformed into electrical energy (the flash).

A Hollywood producer once asked me about fairy dust streaming from the tips of wands. I told him it was nonsense.

WEREWOLVES

The Legend
The werewolf legend is both ancient and simple. Come full moon, certain men (or, more unusually, women) transform into wolves. They roam the countryside doing what wolves do – including killing people – until the moon moves to its next phase. Then they change back to their original form.

Lycanthropy, as the condition is called, is catching. If a werewolf bites you, you're infected and become a werewolf in your turn.

Although the wolf legend is popular throughout Europe, other countries have produced their own *were* lore. China, for example, has a tradition of were-foxes. Japan has were-hares.

The Reality
In parts of Africa, certain secret societies required their members to put on the skin of an animal and mimic its actions. They believed this enabled them to absorb the creature's strength and courage. The idea worked well, at least at the psychological level. Leopard men or lion men became known as ferocious warriors. Superstitious tribespeople, catching a glimpse of

what seemed to be a leopard in the jungle, concluded the sorcerers had learned how to *become* the animal... and the whole *were* legend started.

But this primitive form of imitative magic is not the whole story. It seems there really *is* a wizardry technique that can turn you into something utterly *other*. One variation uses an ancient Chinese system of philosophy called the *I Ching*.

I Ching means 'Book of Changes' and it's widely believed to be the oldest book in the world. All the same, you can still buy yourself a copy (translated!) in most major bookshops.

If you do, you'll quickly discover the *I Ching* is generally used as an oracle. You ask a question, then toss three coins or count a large bundle of dried yarrow stalks. Your manipulations produce a special symbol called a hexagram. You look up the meaning of the hexagram you've created and there's the answer to your question.

Used this way, the *I Ching* is not only harmless, but positively useful. Over the years I've found it a source of intelligent, insightful and relevant advice. But the *I Ching* can be used in other, more magical ways. Some of them are dangerous.

An American travel writer named William

Seabrook discovered just *how* dangerous when he and some friends conducted an experiment in a flat above Times Square. The subject was a Russian émigré he later referred to as Magda. She drew Hexagram No. 49, which is usually translated as 'Revolution'.

I've no idea how the group came across the method they used. It's possible Seabrook stumbled on it during his travels in the Far East. But it was one of the magical methods. As a result, Magda suddenly found herself... elsewhere. 'I'm naked!' she told her startled companions. 'I'm naked underneath a fur coat and I'm running in the snow.' Then, to their horror, she began to growl.

In the Times Square flat, it quickly became obvious that Magda had sunk into a trance. But when Seabrook and his colleagues tried to wake her, she attacked them, growling and snapping like a wild beast.

Magda was a big woman. It took a long time to subdue her. It took longer still for her to come out of the trance. She looked dazed, bewildered and apologetic. She had, she said, been transported to the wilds of her native Russia. 'I became a wolf,' she told them. 'I was running through the snow by the light of a full moon.'

Interestingly, the earliest versions of the *I*

Ching indicate that Hexagram 49 was originally associated with moulting – the process by which an animal sheds its fur in preparation for the growth of a winter coat.

ZOMBIES

The Legend
The zombie legend comes from the Caribbean island of Haiti. Wizards are supposed to use a perverted form of voodoo to raise the dead and set them working in the cane fields. Although your typical zombie is pretty dumb, he can follow simple orders. Cane-cutting isn't exactly rocket science.

Zombies work tirelessly from dawn to dusk, require no pay and while they *do* have to be fed, they aren't choosy about what they eat. You have to be careful, however, not to let them have salt, which breaks the spell and ends their magical enslavement.

The Reality
The roots of the legend are particularly nasty. There have been several well-investigated examples of zombies in Haiti. One concerns Clairvius Narcisse, a forty-year-old peasant who died in hospital, spitting blood, on 2 May 1962.

He was buried next day in a cemetery north of his native village. His family put a heavy concrete slab over his grave.

Eighteen years later he turned up again. After introducing himself to his sister in a market place, he told how, before his death, his brother had contacted a *bokor** because of a land dispute between them. The bokor bewitched Clairvius so that he fell ill and died. After his death he was raised from the grave by a group of men. They beat him and bound him then led him away to work with other zombie slaves in the north of the island. After two years, the slave master was killed and the zombies freed. Narcisse wandered for sixteen years, terrified of his brother. He only returned to his family after hearing of his brother's death.

Bokors make zombies by means of a rite that produces a mysterious powder. Some of the ingredients, like grave dust and dried-up bits of corpses, are revolting but more or less harmless. Others, like *zombie's cucumber*, suggest there may be more than magic involved.

Zombie's cucumber is the plant *datura stramonium*, a poison related to the thorn-apple used in witch's flying ointment. In small doses it

---

* That's a wizard who specialises in making zombies.

causes hallucinations. Take too much and you fall into a stupor and die.

Another ingredient of the bokor's powder is ground blowfish bone. Blowfish is the speciality of Japanese *fugu* restaurants whose patrons like to live on the edge. How far on the edge is illustrated by the fact that blowfish poison is 500 times stronger than cyanide. A lethal dose would scarcely cover the head of a pin. A fragment of bone left in your fillet is enough to kill you, as a handful of fugu patrons discover every year.

To make a zombie, the bokor slips a small dose of his magic powder into your food. Very soon you get sick. Then you fall into a coma that shows all the signs of death. Haiti is a hot country and there's a race to get corpses buried before they begin to rot, so you're likely to be in your grave within a day.

But if the ingredients were properly balanced, you aren't really dead. You're just in a state of suspended animation. Provided the bokor can get to you in time, he can revive you with the proper antidote. You may be suffering brain damage. You'll certainly be stupefied and confused. Either way you'll follow orders.

6
The Secret of the Mystery Name

If that litany of doom hasn't put you off, maybe this will:

An awful lot of magic doesn't work the way you want it to. Some of it doesn't work at all.

I know that's the last thing you want to hear. I know it seems to contradict a lot of what you read in the last chapter. But I promised I'd tell it like it is and that, unfortunately, is *how* it is.

One American wizard had this to say: 'We have... observed... that the efficacy of the Art does not always manifest in a positive way in every practitioner's life.' Which translates as: magic probably won't do you much good. Another went even further. He said he'd never, ever, seen an entirely positive outcome from a spirit conjuration. The spirits came all right, but if you asked them to do something for you, the result was always a mess. Sometimes it was an absolute disaster.

My own experience has been that there are more failed experiments in magic than there are successes. Most wizards know this in their heart of hearts. That's why they often concentrate on magical experiments where there's no way of telling whether they work or not.*

So why do they bother at all?

First off, as you've seen in the last chapter, some magic *does* work. It may even work as advertised. You're not dealing with a science here, with repeatable experiments. You're dealing with an art. The carrot hanging in front of every wizard is the possibility of improving his skill... maybe even to the point where he can get it right every time.

Second, the fact that magic works at all is important. You only need one white crow to prove all crows aren't black. You only need one successful magical experiment to prove the way we normally look at the world is wrong. That's a seductive thought. If we could just understood the process a little better, we *might* end up with repeatable experiments. Even if that never

* One wizard colleague of mine is currently mounting rituals 'to reduce terrorism in the world'. However many terrorist outrages there may be in the future, she can always claim there would have been more without her magic. Other wizards are even more vague. I know one who designed a ritual that would 'open the second watchtower of the hidden universe'. *Purleese!*

happens, we've still increased our understanding of the universe.

(I might mention there's a mischievous element in magic. You get results that convince you you're on the edge of proof. Then something happens that makes it all nonsense. On the other hand, failed experiments are typically followed by a resounding success just when you're about to give up altogether. The same pattern shows itself in psychical research.)

Third, wizard training disciplines the mind and illuminates your inner world in a way that will enrich your life.

That said, you won't become a fully trained wizard from reading this book.* Even the basics take between four and five years of daily exercises. After that you start learning by experience. But you will get some benefits. You will try some interesting experiments. And you will lay a useful foundation for later study in a wizard school.

Still with me after all that sober stuff? Then let's get started on your training.

Students in the Golden Dawn took on a secret Mystery Name. Inside the school they were no longer called Fred Bloggs. Instead, they were known

---

* Or any other book, come to that.

as Frater (Brother) or Soror (Sister) followed by the Mystery Name. So Aleister Crowley became *Frater Perdurabo*, MacGregor Mathers, who was one of the founders, became *Frater S'Rhioghail Mo Dhream* and W. B. Yeats, who headed the school for a time, became *Frater Daemon Est Deus Inversus.*

I can tell you these Mystery Names because the people who used them are all dead. But in their time, nobody knew the names, not even other members of the school. When you introduced yourself, or signed a magical document, you only used the initial letters. So Crowley was known as *Frater P.*, Mathers as *Frater S.R.M.D.* and Yeats as *Frater D.E.D.I.*

You can see from the examples that Mystery Names weren't really names at all. If anything they were more like mottos. *Perdurabo* is Latin and means 'I will endure'. *Daemon Est Deus Inversus* is also Latin and means 'the devil is the reverse side of God'. *S'Rhioghail Mo Dhream* is Gaelic and translates as 'royal is my race'. Other members of the school used other languages, including English. Sometimes the names got complicated. Mathers had a second secret name that translated as, 'with God as my leader and the sword as my companion'.

All this sounds like a bit of harmless fun, but there's more to it than that. Your Mystery Name is never chosen *for* you, it's chosen *by* you. Which is what I want you to do now.

Go off and meditate about the most intriguing subject in the world – yourself. Try to find the essence of who you are. Think about the sum of your magical ambitions. Look for your most profoundly held belief, your strongest insight. Put it all together and try to find the words (in your native language at this stage) to say what you've discovered.

It took me a short paragraph to give you those instructions, but it's going to take you weeks, months, or even years to carry them out. Don't let that worry you. Above all, *don't skimp on the effort*. Although it sounds straightforward, I can't begin to tell you how important this exercise will be to you.

Self-knowledge is one of life's most valuable gifts. This simple assignment will help you develop it big time. But absolute honesty is vital. You're not trying to pass an exam. You're not trying to impress anybody. Your Mystery Name is never going to be known to anybody but yourself.* So if you discover you're a lying toad, don't go into denial. Deal with it.

The *way* to deal with it is to turn the insight

---

* Even your closest friends should get nothing more than the initials. Tell them it's a wizard tradition – which it is.

into an aspiration. Adopting the name *Frater L.T.* (Lying Toad) will give you some magical authority, if only because it happens to be true. But you'll do even better if you look for a way to fix the fault then use *that* as your magical motto.

For example, you might decide to make your motto *I Will Work Hard to Tell the Truth*. If you positively can't live with being called *Frater I.W.W.H.T.T.T.T.*, translate it into Latin, Gaelic, Greek, Urdu or anything else that looks better.

Basic though it is, this magical exercise is the most important piece of wizardry you'll ever do. But it comes with a health warning. Some years ago I began to notice that when people seriously took on a Mystery Name, God, Life or the Universe insisted they live up to it. The lying toads who pledged they would work hard to tell the truth were faced with opportunity after opportunity to do just that. And if they failed, the lies they told turned around and bit them.

This is odd. It's as if, having set your foot on the wizard path, *something* insists you live up to your ideals. If you don't, you seem to be hammered with test after test until the pain forces you to think again. If you were to press me about the mechanism, I'd guess it has to do with waking up.

There's a magical theory that most people go through life in something very like a dream. They *think* they're awake, but they're not. They *think* they're in charge of what they do, but they're not. They're driven by agendas so well hidden they don't even know they're there. But wizards can't live like that. When you deal with magical currents, it's far too dangerous.

Taking on a Mystery Name announces your decision to become a wizard. At once, something out there starts prodding you to wake up and start living up to the motto you've chosen.

Don't say I didn't warn you.

7
The Magical Art of Memory

Memory training has been part of the magical arts since the Renaissance. You're about to find out why. Read the following passage carefully:

After the light began to appear, the centre was red, an ash colour blush; the circumference blue. The second division green, fiery red and purple. In the third division, the centre was fiery, the inferior waters purple, the superior white. The fourth division was azure blush, the Sun and Moon then appearing pale blush. In the fifth division the earth was red and the centre fiery, the waters blush azure, the Sun and Moon ash colour. The sixth division of the earth was a red blush, the centre fiery.*

Cover the passage with your hand and recite it aloud from memory.

You can't, can you? You probably can't even

* Quoted from *The Rosie Crucian Secrets*, by Dr John Dee, Aquarian Press, 1985.

remember the colour of the inferior waters in the third division. (Don't strain: it's purple.)

Now imagine your life depended on reciting from memory scores of passages as complicated as that one *without once making a mistake*. Think of that. Just one slip and you're dead. Your family will find your hideously mutilated body tomorrow.

That's the situation wizards were in a few centuries ago. They had books of rituals that promised all sorts of magical results. But they firmly believed one slip could lead to disaster. Every ceremony had to be word-perfect. And carried out from memory.

There are wizards I know today who aren't so careful. Maybe they don't use such dangerous rituals any more. But even if you can get away with reading aloud from a book, the ritual itself loses something. It's like going to a play where the actors walk around with scripts in their hands. So the first art you learn as a wizard is the Art of Memory.

There are lots of ways to improve your memory – I wrote a whole book on them once – but the one I'm going to teach you is the traditional wizard's way. It dates back to Ancient Greece and it began with a disaster.

The date was around 500 BC. The man was

Simonides of Ceos, which is a small island in the Aegean. Simonides wasn't strictly a wizard, but he *was* a poet and the two aren't very different. In late middle age, he was at the height of his fame. Twenty years earlier he'd written the first known lyrical ode in honour of Olympic Games winners. That was a bit like writing a really great pop song today. It got you noticed.

Although born in Ceos, Simonides spent most of his life in Athens – and in good company. He was closely associated with at least three rulers. In those days, who you knew was important. Most poets survived because of patronage. Simonides was no exception, but his work eventually became so popular people began to offer him commissions. He was something of a celebrity. He got himself invited to banquets.

It was at one of them that the disaster happened.

The victory banquet was elaborate. It ran to scores of courses and several hundred people attended. At some point in the evening, Simonides was called away. He got back to a scene of horror. In his absence, the floor of the banquet hall had given way, part of the building had collapsed and most of his fellow guests were dead. Many of the bodies were so badly crushed, nobody could recognise them. Someone asked Simonides to help.

It seemed like an impossible task. Hundreds of people had attended the banquet. But as Simonides stood surveying the carnage, he found himself remembering how it had been such a short time ago when the banquet was in full swing. And as he pictured the scene, he realised that by looking at the picture in his mind he could tell where each guest had been seated. Then, by comparing his mental seating plan to the location of the bodies, he could identify each corpse.

It wasn't so much a prodigious feat of memory as a prodigious feat of visualisation. But Simonides was sharp enough to realise he'd stumbled on the makings of a memory aid of astonishing power. He took a break from poetry and soon worked it into a full-scale memory system.

The Simonides system was so effective, it soon spread throughout scholarly circles in Greece. With their admiration for Greek culture, the Romans adopted it as well. But the fall of the Roman Empire marked the collapse of the Classical Civilisations. The Dark Ages began. Much ancient learning was lost – among it Simonides' system of memory training.

History tells you it was the monks who kept the lamp of learning alight – if only just – by preserving many of the ancient books. But wizards played their part as well. Wizards believe, by and large, that there are a great many magical secrets buried in our distant past. More to the point, wizards search for them. At some stage, certainly no later than the Renaissance, they stumbled on Simonides' Art of Memory.

I've already told you why a good memory system was so urgently needed. But there were other things that added to its appeal. Successful wizardry depends almost entirely on a trained mind, particularly a mind trained to visualise vividly. Which was exactly what the Simonides system did. What's more, it delivered instant, measurable results for your visualisation practice

– which is a lot more than you'll get from most magical techniques when you're at the learning stage.

So the Magical Art of Memory was born. This is how it works:

First, you have to find yourself a *locus*. The term is Latin and just means 'place'. But in the Art of Memory, a locus is the visualised equivalent of a physical place. For Simonides, the physical place was the banquet hall where he enjoyed the company of his fellow guests. His locus was the mental picture he built up when asked to identify the bodies. With the flowering of the Renaissance, you were likely to find wizards wandering through large public buildings in every European capital. Their eyes were watchful. They were creating their own private loci. You can do the same.

You may end up in a large public building eventually, but to start off with I'd suggest you use your own home. It may be small,* but it will allow you to practise and it has a priceless additional benefit. Because you live there, you can visualise it vividly already.

Build your locus strongly. Imagine you are walking through your own home. It's essentially a daydream, but make it as detailed as possible.

* Or it may not, of course.

Start at your front door. Note the colour, the number of panels, where you find the knocker or the bell. Open the door and step into the hall. What do you find there? Is there an umbrella stand? A wall mirror? A pot plant? What's the colour of the carpet?

Walk (mentally) through the rest of your house, noting that same degree of detail. Try to follow a logical route. Visit each of the downstairs rooms in turn before moving upstairs. Visit each bedroom in turn. Do all this a few times until the daydream becomes second nature to you. When you can close your eyes anywhere and mentally walk through your home without hesitation, you'll know you've built a working locus.

This is how you use it. The following list is composed of random items that happen to be near me as I sit. I'd like you to read through it once, then follow the instructions.

Pen... mobile phone... beaker... notepad... quartz crystal... spectacles... photograph... book... letter opener... computer... Buddha figure... dragon... candle... toad... coin... magnifying glass... cat... light bulb... iPod... fan... chair.

Cover the list, then write down as many of the items as you can remember. When you've finished, check your list against the original then make a note of how many you recalled correctly. There are twenty-one items on the original list. Most people will remember between seven and ten of them. A few will do better. Almost nobody will remember the whole twenty-one. The note you've just made will be useful for comparison later on.

Now try recalling the same list using the wizard's Art of Memory. Go mentally to the front door of your locus. Leave the pen lying on the doorstep. Open the door and put the mobile phone down immediately inside. You can balance the beaker on the hatstand, stick the notepad on the mirror, glue the quartz crystal to the handle of the living-room door.

Keep walking through your locus the way you've practised, placing items down until you've finished the whole list. Make sure you leave them somewhere you'd notice when you walk this way again. If that proves tricky, try exaggerating the size of the item. Make the pen a giant pen, so you have to climb over it to get through the front door. Do the same with other items if need be. If you find yourself running out of space, it's okay to leave more than one thing in the same room. Just make sure they're both noticeable.

Note I didn't tell you to remember anything. You don't have to. Once you leave things in your locus, you can find them again just by walking through it. Try it. There's the pen on the doorstep... the mobile phone just inside... the beaker on the hatstand... the notepad on the mirror... Write down each one as you find it. Compare with the original list. I'd be astonished if you didn't find you do far better this time than you did before.

With a bit of practice, using your locus will let you memorise any list like that perfectly. And retain it for as long as you like. You can impress people by reciting the list backwards (walk through your locus in reverse order). You can even name a numbered item from the list – sixth, tenth, eighteenth or whatever. Simply walk through counting.

Play about with your locus. Get used to it. Build a bigger one if you want. (Your nearest museum could be a good basis.) Draw up a few more lists and memorise them for fun. At this stage you won't be using your locus to help with magical rituals, but you can use it in other ways. Try memorising your next shopping list instead of writing it down.

Strict use of a locus is only the start, of course. Once you get the hang of it, you'll find visualisation can be used in several different ways to aid your memory. You might, for example, convert numbers into something easier to visualise using simple rhymes:

Zero = hero; 1 = bun; 2 = shoe; 3 = tree; 4 = door; 5 = hive; 6 = sticks; 7 = heaven; 8 = gate; 9 = wine.

Learn that and you can visualise every number you'll ever need. (Ten = a bun being eaten by a hero, of course. Eleven is two buns side by side. Twelve is a bun beside a shoe. And so on.) You can even remember mathematical formulae by placing these items in their correct positions and visualising the result. Try memorising phone numbers, or the value of pi to seventeen decimal places. Create your personal list of PIN numbers. You can store them alongside the thing they refer to in a cupboard in your locus.

As you find out how useful a locus can be, you'll dream up more and more ways of using it. Want to remember somebody's name? Build a special Personnel Room in your locus and store people in it, clearly labelled. Want to remember Latin words? Open up a Roman Room in your locus, break the Latin term into parts you can visualise, then link those parts visually with the meaning of the word. For example, the Latin word pater means 'father'. Break the Latin down into bits you can visualise: pat her. Now go to your Roman Room and visualise your father *patting* the head of a young girl (pat her). Sounds silly, but it works.

The more often you use it, the better it works. Which will encourage you to use it more. Which will make it work better. Which will... but you get the idea.

While you're earning yourself a reputation as a memory whizz, you're laying down a firm foundation for more wizard's work. You've already learned that a vivid imagination is important in magic and imagination is the mental equivalent of a muscle. The more you exercise it, the stronger it gets.

8
Drinking from the Well of Wisdom

It's three a.m. on a still summer's night. A hooded figure makes his way across a narrow wooden bridge. He wears black robes with a golden cord, the symbol of his standing as a wizard.

The bridge leads to a tiny island that features a building no larger than a summerhouse. There is a glow of candlelight from its window. The figure knocks gently on the door. After a moment, a voice invites him in.

There is a single circular room inside the wooden building. Floor cushions have been strewn around the wall. Near the centre is a low table on which burns a lone candle. Beside it, seated cross-legged, is a second robed and hooded figure.

'Are the Wards secure?' the first man asks.

The seated figure begins to stand up. 'The Wards are secure, Brother,' he says. Then he yawns, stretches and walks off across the bridge into the night. The first man shuts the door, and takes his place beside the little table. He closes his eyes, but he is not asleep. He has sworn to remain awake until six a.m. Despite appearances, he is keeping watch. But in a wizard way.

All this is going on in the grounds of a small hotel in Britain. On a normal week, it would be packed with holiday-makers and business people. For most of the year it has coped with the usual run of weddings and conferences. It's a new hotel, no more than nine or ten years old. Its staff are professional and discreet. Not one of its usual guests suspects it was built on the instructions of a spirit.

The entity was one of those higher Beings who get in touch with wizards from time to time. It suggested (by telepathy) that the time was ripe for a magical business. It had to be set up on ethical principles. It had to serve the community. It had to provide a setting where people could grow spiritually. A small hotel seemed ideal.

The wizard in question, a young man with no hotel experience, protested that it had to make money as well. The spirit told him not to worry about stuff like that. The wizard and his wife went into partnership with two other couples. They raised money, mainly by mortgaging their homes, and hired builders. The spirit gave advice at all stages of the project. It also advised on how the hotel should be run.

With such a background, it's not surprising the management was sympathetic to the needs of their fellow wizards. The current group had taken over the entire hotel for a week. They needed privacy to practise their magic.

But not just physical privacy. The wizards preferred not to be disturbed by astral entities. They wanted no one snooping in their minds. So the first thing their head wizard did was establish the Guardians of the Quarters.

The form that Quarter Guardians take depends partly on a wizard's training, partly on what they're needed for. John Clelland, the wizard mentioned in our first chapter, would probably have called the four archangels Raphael, Michael, Gabriel and Auriel. A closely allied tradition uses the Kerubim: a Winged Man, a Winged Lion, an Eagle and a Winged Bull. In Iceland, the traditional Guardians are a Dragon, a Rock Giant, a Bull and a Bird.

But whatever the form, the principle is the same. As a magician, you use your imagination to create a figure. You establish it in a particular quarter – East, South, West or North. You visualise it vividly and in detail. If you do your job properly, the spiritual essence of the figure flows in to give it life. Once that happens, you can safely leave the creature alone. It will faithfully stand guard over the direction in which you placed it.

The head wizard didn't use any of the Guardians I've mentioned. She was an unusual woman. Her training included witchcraft, which she sometimes mixed with Egyptian, Greek and other ancient rites to create a powerful magical brew. On this occasion, she picked four particularly potent Guardians from the pagan tradition.

To call them, she first went to the easternmost part of the hotel grounds. There, facing the eastern horizon, she carefully built up the imaginary figure of a gigantic Stag. When the figure was firmly in place, she called to it aloud: 'Cernunnos of the Twelve Tines, I bid thee welcome! Grant a blessing on our work in this place and keep us from harm.' The creature turned towards her. The spontaneous movement showed the spiritual essence had flowed in.

From there, the wizard moved to the south and built up the towering shape of a beautiful white horse. 'Epona, White Mare of the Hills, I bid thee welcome! Grant a blessing to our work in this place and keep us from interruption.' The creature turned towards her.

Next, she walked to the westernmost quarter of the grounds. There she visualised a giant cow. 'Mona, Sacred Cow of the Sacred Isles,* I bid thee welcome! Grant a blessing to our work in this place and guard us well.' The creature turned towards her.

Finally she went north to create the imaginary shape of an enormous bear. 'Artor, Great Bear, Lord of Logres,' she called out. 'I bid thee welcome. Lay a blessing upon our work in this place and grant us peace in heart, mind and body.' The creature turned towards her.

By the time this work was done, the inner levels of the hotel grounds were guarded by Cernunnos, Epona, Mona and Artor, four mythic pagan creatures of great power. Although partly the wizard's creation, they were also alive in their own right. They would continue to stand

* The 'Sacred Isles' are the British Isles in Western magical tradition.

guard over their particular areas until dismissed when the wizards' work was done. They would repel magical attack from any of the four directions – East, South, West or North. More importantly, they would make sure there were no astral interruptions.*

All the same, any defence can be broken by a superior force. The head wizard was a careful woman. During the day while she was awake she could check out the four Wards from time to time simply by turning her attention towards them. But what of when she was asleep? She called her fellow wizards together and asked for volunteers. Starting at sunset (which was around nine p.m. at that time of year) each was to take responsibility for a three-hour shift during which he or she regularly monitored the four Guardians.

This was the volunteer's sole duty. He went to the little meditation building on the island and lit a candle if one was not already burning. Then at intervals of no more than fifteen minutes – fewer if he wished – he would close his eyes and, in his imagination, walk the boundaries of the hotel grounds. This *astral walk*, as the process was called, enabled him to

* The term *astral* is often used by wizards of the Western Esoteric Tradition to describe places, things or entities that exist in the world of the imagination.

check that the Guardians were still in place and undisturbed. In the unlikely event that they were under attack, he was instructed to support them. If they faced a really serious attack, he would call reinforcements.

So it went until dawn. Each volunteer remained in the meditation building until relieved of his duties by the next in line. If the next in line was late, or forgot altogether, the incumbent was sternly instructed to stay put. The wizards took magical security very seriously.

But what was the wizard work that demanded such security?

With the Wards in place, the wizards began their preparation for an important ritual. The first thing they did was to select their robes.

A wizard's robe is a little like the surplice worn by Christian clerics and a lot like the monastic robes worn by monks. It may or may not be hooded. It hangs to the ankle and is secured by a soft cord girdle, again much like a monk's. The likelihood is that it will be either all black or all white. Some wizards do wear more brightly coloured robes – red seems to be a favourite – but these usually show their office in a particular school, as do elaborate embroidery, sashes and other decorations.

The basic robe, the working robe, serves a

special purpose that has nothing to do with office. It allows you to put on your *magical personality*. Since you've read this far in *The Wizard's Apprentice*, you'll know that magic works from the inside out. In other words, it starts with your mind.

When wizards aren't being wizards, their minds work like anybody else's (more or less). Before they can do successful magic, they have to change that. They have to get into the right mindset. Which is where the robe comes in. If you try to work magic while wearing your ordinary clothes, all the cares of your day come crowding in. You find yourself worrying about your mother or thinking of the money you owe.

Pull a robe over your head and it shuts all that out. With a robe on, you look the business. More importantly, you *feel* the business. You feel like a wizard; and it focuses your mind. Some wizards use special 'magical' rings, necklaces, lamens, talismans or what have you to achieve the same effect. But the robe is always the main thing.

Robed and ready, their feet slippered or, in a few cases, bare, the wizards proceeded to prepare their place of working. In this instance, their place of working was a large, carpeted room inside the hotel. At other times other guests used it for business meetings and conferences. This, to a wizard, meant it needed to be cleaned. Not physically, of course – the hotel staff did that. It needed to be cleaned spiritually and emotionally.

There are several ways of doing this. One is to burn a little sage and fumigate the room with the smoke. That's a trick used by Native American wizards, who roll the sage into convenient, cigar-shaped bundles and light one end.*

The wizards in the hotel favoured another method, however. They scrubbed the inner levels of the room with geometrical figures known as pentagrams. They set up a ring of fire and established Wards within the Wards. This time the Archangels were called to stand guard. All of it happened in the imagination of the group. Those familiar with the rite moved about the room with grace and confidence as they created the proper visualisations.

Wards within Wards were, perhaps, a bit of overkill. But wizards look on their place of working the same way surgeons look on an operating theatre. If you're going to do the job safely, everything needs to be disinfected. You can't be too careful.

Now came the reason for it all. The wizards had gathered to perform a special rite. In some

---

* You can buy bundles like this in health shops and New Age stores today. They're called *smudge sticks*.

ways it was experimental magic, something that hadn't been tried before. Various elements of the rite were familiar. It was the way they were combined that was different.

It began with a ritual drama.

Ritual dramas are fairly common in modern magic. They're usually a re-enactment of some ancient myth, chosen because of its effect on the mind. This one was based on the legend of King Arthur and his Knights of the Round Table. It revolved around the search for the Holy Grail. Like actors in a play, wizards took the parts of King Arthur, Queen Guinevere, Galahad, Lancelot, several other knights, and the magician Merlin. Like actors in a play, they spoke their lines and carried out specific actions. Those not directly involved sat and watched, like an audience.

But at a certain point, the focus switched away from the drama. Curtains were drawn to darken the room and the Wizard Merlin led the entire group in what's technically known as a *pathworking*.

Pathworkings used to be one of the most closely guarded secrets in wizardry. Every school had its own collection. Most schools still do; and most schools still keep some to themselves. A pathworking is a guided meditation. Those who take part are led on an inner journey full of mystic incidents and symbols.

Usually, every detail of a pathworking is worked out and scripted in advance. The result can be a hefty document running to as many pages as a small book. But in this instance the group was attempting something different. The robed Merlin figure began speaking softly:

Close your eyes.

As you sit in the darkness, utterly relaxed, I want you to smell the smoke. This is wood smoke, mixed with the heavier acrid smell of burning turf or dung. Catch it in your nostrils. Feel it in your throat. It's all around you, stinging your eyes in the darkness. I want you to make every effort to smell that smoke.

As the smoke catches in your throat, you will become aware of its source: a mean little fire, nearly out. Just a few dully glowing embers, hardly enough to cast light into this little cottage.

As you stare at the glow, waiting for your eyes to adjust, try to become aware of the other smells masked by the smell of smoke. The smell of old straw. The smell of human sweat and urine. The smell of damp. Animal smells. Earth smells.

It's cold. Not biting chill, but cold. And because it's cold, you become gradually aware of the body heat of your companions. I want you to sense these things, search them out: the smells, the cold, the faint glow of the near-dead fire, the body heat of your companions.

If you look up, you can just make out a smoke-blackened beam above. Not cut wood, just a thick branch from the forest. There is a faint grey light creeping through a crack in the rough wooden shutters over the only window.

Your eyes are beginning to adjust. The floor of the cottage is dried mud with a light scattering of rushes. There is sacking covering the only door in a tattered curtain.

When you are ready, I want you to move as a group to the door and select someone to open it. When he or she does so, I shall tell you what you see...

He waited until someone said quietly that the door had been opened, then went on:

It is daylight, but overcast, threatening rain with a chill breeze and the fresh clean scent of grass. The cottage behind you is a mean, mud-walled building roofed with stone slabs and sods of turf. You are standing near a well-trodden roadway which winds up a hillside to the towers and turrets of a castle at the top. Even from this distance you can see gaily coloured pennants flying above its battlements.

There is a great deal of activity around the castle. Pilgrims, horsemen, even beggars seem to be able to gain admittance.

Behind you, curling behind the cottage and leading away somewhere behind the hill, is a rough, stony track.

There the Merlin figure stopped. From this point, the group was on its own. They had to follow their imaginary adventure without any further guidance, trusting their skills as wizards to lead them in the right direction.

It should have been chaos. Here was a group of people who were following their own daydreams. The only thing they had in common was the starting point. Every one should have gone off in a different direction, making up his own story. But it didn't happen that way. Although acting entirely within their own imaginations, the wizards stayed together as a group. Their inner eyes saw the same landscapes, the same buildings, the same trees, the same people.

They agreed quietly on the places they wanted to go. When they went there, they saw the same sights. By the end of the experiment, when they had all returned to their starting point and opened their eyes, they had all had the same experience. They'd met with a lady, talked to her and accepted her gifts.

You could think of that experience in different ways. You might decide the lady was a spirit who gave the wizards advice. Or you might think she was something they created together, like a character in a story. Or you might imagine she was an aspect of their deeper selves – what psychologists call an *archetype*.

Much of wizardry is like that – encounters in the world of the imagination. Often what they are is not exactly understood. They don't make you rich. They don't make you powerful. They don't help you produce spectacular effects. But wizards still think they're important. When they practise the magic of the imagination, they firmly believe the things they see and do will make them better people. Experience has taught them they are drinking from the well of wisdom.

9
The Pendulum
Your Pocket Guide

Some kids spend years wondering what they'll do when they grow up. Nobody tells them most adults spend years wondering much the same. The problem is acute for wizards, who need to know themselves in order to practise magic safely. Knowing what you want is a major part of knowing yourself. It's also a lot harder than you'd think. Remember that sinking feeling as you mutter, 'But on the other hand...'.

What is it you really, really, *really* want?

Fortunately help's at hand. Some time in the sixteenth century,* wizards invented a magical tool as useful as a wand, but less well known. It helped them understand themselves, distinguish right from wrong, discover lost treasure, track down ghosts, learn secrets and a host of other useful things.

---

* Maybe earlier – it's difficult to be sure.

The tool was a pendulum. You can make one.

All you need is a weight and something to hang it on – string, thread, wire, chain. People get very fancy about pendulums. I've seen them beautifully carved from wood or crafted from rock crystal. But most of the frills are wasted. It's how you use a pendulum that counts, not the way it's made.

(That said, if the weight is pointed at the end you get a more accurate reading. And if you plan to use it outdoors, you don't want to make it too light, otherwise it blows about in the wind.)

Contrary to what you've heard, a pendulum won't let you talk to ghosts or Hidden Masters or flying saucer aliens from the planet Zog. All it does is let you talk to yourself. But that's enough.

Pause now for a lightning lesson on the human mind.

The part of your mind you're aware of, the part that chatters inside your head, isn't all of you. In fact, it isn't even most of you. Outside your conscious mind there's a huge *other* mind most people never get to know at all.

It's a mind that tells your heart to beat. It's a mind that sends you bright ideas. It's a mind that stores things you've forgotten. It's a mind that was grown-up before you were born and a mind that will (maybe) survive when you're dead. It's a mind that seems to exist outside time and space so it has information you don't have. It's your wise mind. It's the mind that interests wizards.

A pendulum will let you talk to it. More to the point, a pendulum will let it answer. But first you have to set things up.

Draw a circle with a cross through it on a piece of paper, like this:

Prop your elbow on the table and hold your pendulum over the centre of the circle, like this:

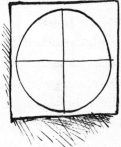

Note you're holding the string/thread/chain/whatever between your thumb and forefinger, so the pendulum swings freely. Actually, you may find it swings a bit too freely. Be patient and give it time to settle down so it hangs quite still above your drawing.

Basically, your pendulum can swing in four different directions:

1. In a circle, clockwise.
2. In a circle, anticlockwise.
3. Side to side, moving across you.
4. Up and down, moving away from and towards you.

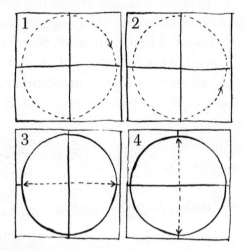

What you have to do is find out what each of these movements means when it comes to answering your questions. There are four possibilities (obviously):

1. Yes.
2. No.
3. I don't know.
4. I don't want to answer.

You *could* simply assign whichever answer you fancy to whatever movement you want. But experienced wizards advise against it. They say you'll always get better results if you let the pendulum (i.e. your other mind) tell you. Here's how you do that:

Use your pendulum to make each of the four movements in turn. Do this purposely. It only takes a slight movement of your fingers to swing it round clockwise. Then let it come to a halt and swing it round anticlockwise. Do this until you've made all four swinging movements.

Now comes the interesting bit. Hold your pendulum quite still over the centre of the circle and ask out loud, 'Which direction means *Yes?*' Then wait. *You are not to move the pendulum.* Just wait. Keep your eye on the pendulum, but don't move it.

If nothing happens after a reasonable time, repeat the question mentally. 'Which direction means *Yes?*' Or, you might try putting it this way: 'My other mind will now decide which of these four pendulum movements will mean *Yes* in answer to my questions.'

You should get a reaction from the pendulum within seconds. But if you don't, repeat the word *Yes* mentally over and over for a few moments. If *that* doesn't do the trick, have a friend ask the question for you. The one thing you definitely, positively, absolutely must not do is move the pendulum. Trust me, it will move all by itself.

Once the pendulum has shown you which movement represents *Yes*, ask which movement represents *No* and again wait for an answer. Repeat the process until you've discovered the meanings of all four movements. In every case, the pendulum moves of its own accord to tell you.

Except, of course, it doesn't. Many years ago, wizards believed it did. They believed the pendulum contained a magical force that made it move and when that stopped making sense, they started to believe it was being moved by spirits. Nowadays, wizards buy into the scientific explanation. What you really have here is something called an *ideo-motor response*. You may not *think* you're moving the pendulum. It may not *feel* as if you're moving the pendulum. But that's really what's happening all the same.

Tiny, tiny movements of your muscles – so small you're not even aware of them – are what actually move the pendulum. But what *directs* the movement is your other mind. Psychologists call your other mind the subconscious or the unconscious. This gives the impression of something that lies *below* your conscious mind and so is inferior. Which is why I prefer the term 'other mind'. In my experience there are aspects of your other mind that are actually *superior* to anything your conscious mind can manage.

The fact that your other mind is able to pick directions for its answers shows three things:
1. It can hear what you say (not to mention what's in your thoughts).
2. It can think and reason.
3. It can direct the movement of the pendulum.

But that's just the start. Because your other mind seems to know things you don't. I've no idea how it manages this, but experience will show you that it does. In a moment I want you to try a few little experiments to prove this, but before you do, I want you to make one more set of wizard tools – a pair of dowsing rods. This is almost as easy as making a pendulum and while the rods aren't as versatile as a pendulum, since they only really help you locate water, they will quickly help you prove for yourself what I've been saying about your other mind.

The first time I saw a dowser at work, he made himself a dowsing rod by cutting a forked branch from a tree. (Hazel is the traditional wood.) But the forked rod isn't all that easy to learn how to use, while the rods I'm going to tell you how to make can be used successfully, first time, by nearly everybody.

All you need are a couple of wire coat-hangers, the sort that come back with your dry cleaning, and a pair of pliers, or similar wire-cutters.

Now follow the diagrams:

Step One

Start with your basic wire coat-hanger

Step Two

Untwist, so it begins to open out

Step Three

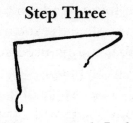

Bend into a rough L-shape

Step Four

Use wire-cutters to trim the ends

Now do the same thing with the other coat-hanger.

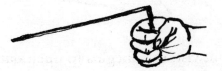

See? Now you've got a set of high-quality, professional-standard dowsing rods. You hold each one like this:

And you hold them both parallel to each other, like train tracks. Now take yourself and your rods out into your garden, if you have one, or your yard, or street or whatever open space is outside your house. Have a look round. I'm guessing you have no idea where your water main runs. But your other mind knows and you're just about to prove it.

Hold your rods out in front of you, still parallel to each other. Walk slowly up and down in a grid pattern so you cover the space outside your house. When you walk over the water main (or any other underground watercourse, like a subterranean stream or river) your rods will cross. They'll do this entirely of their own accord, although you now know they're actually controlled by your other mind... which somehow knows where to find underground water.

(If you can't be bothered to make proper rods, you can get exactly the same effect by straightening two paper clips, bending them into an L shape and inserting the short leg into the caps from two ballpoint pens. You use them as above and they react in the same way, crossing when you pass over water.)

Some wizards claim you can use rods to find metals as well. Since this includes precious metals like gold, silver and platinum, it could be worth your while finding out if you have the knack. Here's how you test it:

While you're out of the room, have a friend hide a coin underneath the carpet or mat, making sure it doesn't show. To find it, you'll need your rods and another coin of the same denomination. Hold the coin in one hand and use the rods as you would to find water. With the coin in your hand, they'll now cross when they pass over a sample of the same metal, and not just water.

Scientists have a rational explanation for water dowsing. They say that burying a water main leaves very subtle traces, while natural underground springs have particular geological features. You may not notice them, but your highly observant other (subconscious) mind does and moves the rods accordingly.

Dowsing for metals is a bit more spooky, but the rationalists suspect it works in much the same way. But this explanation will crash and burn when you start to use your pendulum.

The pendulum takes dowsing on to a whole other level.

For a start, you can use it like a friend and ask it for advice. The only thing you have to remember is to frame your questions so they're susceptible to a YES or NO answer. Something like *Should I turn left or right here?* simply won't hack it. It's also as well to realise you don't have to *take* the advice. You always remain the one who's responsible for your actions.

If you find the advice is generally useful, you might try asking it to predict the future. You'll still only get YES/NO answers so you need to be very creative in framing your questions.

But however creative you are, I have to admit the pendulum won't give accurate predictions for everybody... or even for most people. It seems to depend on a personal talent for prediction, something that's relatively rare. What the pendulum does is let you tap the talent. Since it's perfectly possible you're a prophet and don't know it, experimenting with the pendulum in this way could be very worthwhile.

When you've played around for a bit, made yourself really familiar with the way the pendulum works, you're ready to try one of the creepiest of all pendulum experiments – map dowsing. This is the technique that let the archaeologist Tom Lethbridge find hitherto undiscovered megalithic sites. This is the technique that directs wizards towards buried treasure. This is the technique that allows you to explore for oil, locate lost objects or people.

Here again, not everyone can manage it, but

unlike pendulum prediction, it's not all that rare. Decide what you're looking for – megalithic sites, treasure, whatever – then spread a large-scale map on the table. It has to be large-scale (a good Ordnance Survey is ideal) otherwise the pendulum can't narrow things down and will indicate ridiculous locations like the whole of London for you to search.

Rest your elbow on the table, dangle your pendulum and ask it to locate your target item. Then slowly criss-cross the map in a grid pattern until you get a YES reaction. Make careful note of the map coordinates, then get out in the real world and check to see if your pendulum was right.

For people like Lethbridge – and you might well be one of them – map dowsing can be consistently accurate. Unlike dowsing for water, there is no rational explanation.

It's just good old wizardry at work.

10
The Haunting

A tradition in the magical community has it that the Old Testament king Solomon was a wizard.

There's little indication of this in the Bible, but the Qu'ran and an ancient Ethiopian holy book, the *Kebra Negast* (Glory of Kings), are more forthcoming. They describe how he had visions of events at a distance, how he could converse with every type of animal and insect in its own language and how he used a lapwing to carry messages, in much the same way that Harry Potter uses an owl.

According to the *Kebra Negast*, when Mekeda, the Queen of Sheba* made her famous visit to Solomon, he tricked her into sleeping with him with the result that she went home pregnant. She subsequently gave birth to a son called Menylek.

---

* There's considerable controversy about where the country of Sheba was actually located, but the *Kebra Negast* equates it firmly with what's now Ethiopia.

When Menylek grew up, he visited his father and returned to Ethiopia with the Ark of the Covenant, the great magical and religious artefact that had been in Solomon's possession at the time. Solomon aided Menylek's homeward journey by levitating his caravan in a magical manner. The ancient record describes this in the following terms:

Then they loaded the wagons, the horses and the mules in order to depart, and they set out on their journey and they continued to travel on... And no man hauled his wagon, but whether it was men, horses, mules or loaded camels, each was raised above the ground to the height of a cubit,* and all those who rode upon beasts were lifted up along with the beasts to the height of one span of a man. And every one travelled in the wagons like a ship on the sea when the wind bloweth, like a bat through the air and like an eagle when his body glideth above the wind. Thus did they travel.†

Solomon's own method of travel was even more impressive. He flew through the air on a carpet of green silk carried along by the wind according to his orders. The carpet was big

---

* That's the length of your forearm from the elbow to the tip of your middle finger.
† *Kebra Negast*, Brooks Translation, Red Sea Press, 1996.

enough to take his servants as well as himself and an enormous flock of birds flew above it to protect its occupants from the sun.

But the most persistent rumour about Solomon's magical powers is concerned with his ability to control djinn, mischievous spirits that can take on various human and animal forms. There are endless tales about djinn in Arab folklore and the stories of the *Arabian Nights* are full of them. If you've ever read about Aladdin and his marvellous lamp, you've read about a djinn, although it was probably spelled *genie*. It was the creature who emerged to grant Aladdin's wishes when the lamp was rubbed.

Solomon was supposed to have been able to control unruly djinn. Those that misbehaved were imprisoned in vessels of brass, locked by means of Solomon's Seal, incorporated in a magical ring he wore.

Solomon's Seal looked like this, according to one of the ancient grimoires:*

The six-pointed star in the middle, comprising two interlaced equilateral triangles, is also known as the *Megan David* (Star of David) and appears on the flag of Israel to this day.

* The notorious 'black books of magic' that circulated throughout the Middle Ages and into the Renaissance.

I've only ever come across one djinn – a confused creature that somehow wandered into a voodoo ceremony I attended in Philadelphia. It was smaller – and a whole lot less powerful – than Aladdin's towering servant; and didn't look much like him either. The genie of the lamp is usually pictured as a gigantic human figure, bearded and turbaned. The djinn in Philadelphia appeared to the inner sight as a knee-high desert whirlwind. It was, however, capable of talking (through a medium). It explained how it had lost its way on the inner levels and was attracted by the power generated in the voodoo rite. The presiding priestess sent it home.

But if djinns are rare, at least in Western wizardry, the linkage between spirits and magical rings is a little more common. Pope Honorius III (1216–27) had a fearsome reputation as a wizard. A rather nasty black book – the *Constitution of Honorius* – is attributed to him (although some scholars maintain he never wrote it) and he was supposed to have kept a spirit in his signet ring. He chatted to the creature after dark while the walls of the Vatican shook from the release of magical power.*

Closer to home, a wizard of my acquaintance used a magical ring to halt the activities of an

---

* Needless to say, the Catholic Church dismisses the stories about Honorius as total nonsense.

ancient spirit that had begun to haunt him. Both the haunting and its resolution are particularly interesting since they illustrate the difference between fictional and real-life wizardry.

In fiction, the wizard typically calls up a spirit using an arcane rite and a magic circle. A mistake in the rite – or in the drawing of the circle – allows the spirit to escape from the magician's control and cause him endless trouble thereafter.

In this (real-life) case, the haunting happened very differently.

The wizard concerned was a professional writer – a combination of interests more common than you'd imagine. (The scholar Robert Graves somewhere makes the point that in the classical world, poets and magicians were more or less the same things.) I'll call him James, which isn't the name he's known by. Like many wizards he's secretive about his magical activities... especially when they go wrong.

At some stage during the 1980s, James set out to write a short fantasy story centred on a fictional character he called Nectanebo.

In the story, Nectanebo was a powerful, if somewhat dark, sorcerer. He appeared as a saturnine individual dressed in black, who had discovered the secret of immortality. To give a bit of extra glamour to the character, James imagined him as having been born in Ancient Egypt, where he studied dark arts and eventually became Pharaoh.

In order to bring authenticity to the story, James decided to do a little research into life in Ancient Egypt at around the time Nectanebo was born. And at this point, things took a weird turn.

During the course of his reading, James discovered to his surprise that the name Nectanebo, which he thought he'd simply made up, was an authentic Egyptian name. In fact, there really had been two historical pharaohs called Nectanebo at around the time the fictional Nectanebo was supposed to have lived. They were the only two pharaohs of that name in the entire history of Ancient Egypt.

Intrigued, James began to investigate their lives. It transpired that the two pharaohs were related – uncle and nephew. Nectanebo I, the uncle, was nothing at all like James's fictional Nectanebo. He was a military man who seized the throne by force of arms and held it for only a short time.

But the nephew, Nectanebo II, the last native pharaoh in Egypt, was something else. As James began to dig into his background, he found that *this* Nectanebo had a fearsome reputation as a sorcerer and was even credited in some sources with the ability to part water as the Biblical Moses did at the Red Sea.

James wrote off the identical names and shared interest in sorcery as coincidence. But as his research continued, he realised that as an explanation, coincidence simply wouldn't do. Because the broad facts of Nectanebo II's life exactly coincided with the fictional history James had created for his fictional wizard.

This is just a little less spooky than it sounds. Any psychologist will tell you that the mind is prone to playing some strange tricks. It's possible for you to read something in a book, forget all about it, then dredge it up years later, as a dream, a vision or, in the case of a writer, something you genuinely believe to be your personal creation.

Was this what James had done with Nectanebo? He decided not. The problem with the psychological theory was that Nectanebo II was a very obscure pharaoh. In order to find out the sort of detail that appeared in the story, James would have had to consult rare and difficult sources. The information was simply not something he could have picked up casually.

As a wizard himself, he decided he was subject to a haunting. His concentration on the fictional story had called up the spirit of Nectanebo as effectively as any arcane rite.

James's line of thought illustrates a little-known area of investigation within wizardry itself. Some wizards suspect a three-way connection between spirits, fictional characters and *tulpas*, the Tibetan thought-form creations mentioned earlier in this book.

James decided that this haunting might come in useful. He was, after all, a writer as well as a wizard. If the spirit of an ancient pharaoh was knocking on his head, perhaps it could feed him the inspiration – and information – for a full-length novel about the sorcerer-king.

The idea worked all too well. James wrote his novel, set partly in Egypt, partly in present-day America. But his hopes of a best-seller were quickly dashed. For, having finished the novel, he felt impelled to rewrite it... then rewrite it again and again and again.

At first he had no idea at all what was going on. But the constant rewriting ran so contrary to his usual practice that eventually it dawned on him he was being prompted to rewrite by the shade of the original Nectanebo, who was able to manifest again and again on the typed page so long as James kept writing.

The insight might seem fanciful within our

materialistic culture, but James took it seriously enough to do something about it. Since the spirit had to be controlled, he took a trip to Egypt where he commissioned a jeweller to create a special ring. The body of the ring was silver, a metal sacred to the moon. On it, working to James's specific instructions, the jeweller inscribed ten golden hieroglyphs which spelled out the name *Nectanebo*.

To complete the process, James took the ring to the Temple of Philae, which still incorporates some sacred ruins built to the order of Pharaoh Nectanebo II four centuries before the birth of Christ. There he gently absorbed the restless spirit into the ring he'd had made.

The haunting stopped and James was able to get on with other books.

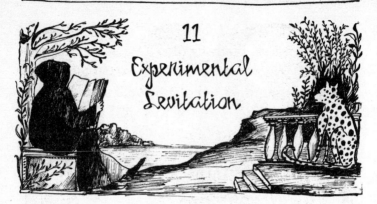

11
Experimental Levitation

Saints and wizards, seldom one and the same, are often credited with the ability to levitate. That's to say, they can rise and float in the air, defying the force of gravity, or sometimes cause other things to do the same.

Most of the levitation stories about saints are well attested. Francis of Assisi, best known for talking to animals, managed the feat many times according to a fellow monk Brother Leo. On at least one occasion he went so high he almost disappeared from sight.

Joseph of Copertino had the embarrassing experience of levitating spontaneously while trying to kiss the Pope's feet. He hovered in the air under the horrified gaze of the assembled Cardinals and Bishops. On another occasion, he was swept up and deposited in the branches of an olive tree, where he was stuck for half an hour until rescued.

Teresa of Avila was prone to levitate while praying, witnessed by several of her nuns. She left a record of what it was like: 'You feel and see yourself carried away you know not whither... I had no power over it... It seemed to me, when I tried to make some resistance, as if a great force beneath my feet lifted me up.'

The main difference between saints and wizards is that levitation just happens to saints – they're usually convinced that God is doing it to them. Wizards try to get the phenomenon under control so they can manage it at will. One of the earliest recorded cases of controlled levitation was that of Simon Magus (Simon the Wizard), a magician from Samaria who lived in the first century AD.

Simon outraged the apostles Peter and John when he offered them hard cash for the secret of their power to transmit the Holy Spirit.* Relations degenerated still further when Simon challenged Peter to a magical battle before an enthusiastic audience in Rome. At the climax of his act, Simon levitated and flew over the city, 'raised up by evil spirits' according to Christian sources. St Peter asked God to put a stop to that nonsense and Simon crashed to his death, or perhaps just got a few broken bones – the records are not altogether clear.

Despite Simon's sorry fate, wizards have been experimenting with levitation ever since. The world-famous 'Scottish Wizard' Daniel Dunglas Home (who was admittedly more of a Spiritualist medium than a magician) achieved some spectacular results on 16 December 1868, when, in the presence of the Earl of Dunraven and several others, he went into trance, floated out through an upstairs window, hovered in the air for a few seconds, then floated back in through another window more than seven feet away.

---

* You can find the whole story in the New Testament, *Acts of the Apostles*, Chapter 8.

Home, who never charged for his demonstrations, was also reported to levitate various objects like tables and heavy furniture.

Oriental wizards, called *fakirs* in India, have a centuries-old tradition of levitation. The great Tibetan yogi Milarepa (*c.*1052–1135) was a wizard long before he became a saint and was supposed to have been so proficient that he could lie down and sleep while in the levitated state.

But not all levitation reports refer to events in the distant past. It's only a few years since the Transcendental Meditation Movement announced that several of its members had managed it and released photographs of grinning adepts seated cross-legged several feet above the ground. It transpired the adepts weren't actually hovering, but had managed to get up there for a split second from a seated position.*

While he was still a teenager, beds levitated in the presence of Matthew Manning, a British psychic and healer who is, at the time of writing, still alive, well and living in Suffolk. For Manning, like the early saints, the phenomenon was spontaneous, but a fellow-countryman, the psychologist Kenneth Batcheldor, followed the wizard's way in that he attempted to get it

---

* Although dismissed by a cynical Press, this is no mean feat. You try jumping in the air while seated cross-legged on the floor.

under control… and succeeded admirably.

Back in the 1960s, Batcheldor became interested in reports of Victorian table-turning. This was something that arose during a Spiritualist craze in the nineteenth century that swept across the Atlantic from America and took the whole of Britain and Europe by storm. For a while, everybody seemed to be holding séances in the hope of contacting the dead. During many of them, heavy tables were reported to move about the room and sometimes even to levitate.

But while the Spiritualist movement survived, table turning didn't. As a séance room phenomenon it gradually died out. Batcheldor decided to find out if he could revive it. He put together a group of people to experiment.

The group met regularly in circumstances similar to a Victorian séance. They'd sit in dim light or complete darkness, their hands on a table and wait patiently for something to happen. But there was one big difference. Batcheldor didn't believe the tables had ever been moved by spirits. He thought it had something to do with the human mind.

It turned out he was right. Without the aid of a medium or any communication from the spirit world, his group eventually managed to get the table to move while being lightly touched, then move without being touched, then levitate in darkness and eventually levitate in daylight with a movie camera trained on it.

The technique Batcheldor used was simple. He discovered that if the group sat in pitch darkness, with absolutely no attempt at scientific control, no rules and no precautions against fraud, strange stuff happened. This would include typical séance-room phenomena like ghostly lights, unexplained sounds and mysterious table movements.

Once he introduced controls – infrared cameras, recording equipment, simple precautions against fraud – the strange stuff stopped. But if he introduced controls very gradually, a little at a time, the phenomena only stopped temporarily. It would come up again, just as strongly, once his sitters got used to the new rules.

More to the point, when the group discovered they could get results under scientifically controlled conditions, the phenomena increased dramatically... to the point where after several months they were able to record their first table levitation.

It became very clear to Batcheldor that persuading something to levitate was just an extension of mentally causing it to move in any way – a process known as *psychokinesis* or PK. (The Russians had a PK medium called Nina Kulagina who was filmed levitating a ball between her hands while concentrating on it fiercely.) Wizards tend to agree and have developed a simple piece of equipment you can make and use to test whether you have the ability yourself.

Before you begin assembling your equipment you'll need a cork, a needle and a square of lightweight silver paper. You might use kitchen foil at a pinch, although it does tend to be a little heavy, but a better thing to use is the foil wrapping found in chocolate biscuit bars, with the tissue-paper backing stripped off.

Take your square of paper and fold it along the diagonals, then unfold it flat. Fold again top to bottom, then unfold and fold side to side. The purpose of all this origami is to produce creases in the paper. If you've done it properly, your square will now look like this:

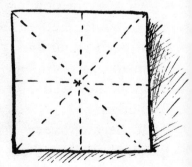

Next, you fold again using the creases as guidelines, but this time you don't flatten

it out, so you end up with a miniature silver tent
that looks like this:

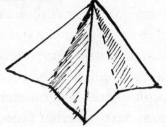

Leave the tent to one side. Take your needle
and embed it in the cork so the eye of the needle
is uppermost:

Finally, balance your tent on top of the needle,
thus:

That's the finished apparatus. What you've

created is a miniature mobile so finely balanced that the slightest force applied will cause it to spin. If you have a talent for PK, that force will be your mind.

To make the test, set up your apparatus on a table top, making sure it's well away from draughts. Now sit a few feet away, place your hands on either side of the device (*without* touching it) and concentrate on spinning the silver tent. Assuming you're PK-positive, what you can expect to happen after a few minutes is a small movement of the tent, like a muscle twitch. Persevere and the tent will begin to spin.

Once you reach this stage, you can begin to play about with your PK powers. Will the spinning to stop and watch what happens. See if you can persuade it to spin in the opposite direction.

If you can seize control of the tent in this way, you can congratulate yourself on exhibiting a rare PK talent, but you're not done yet. With a really finely balanced piece of equipment, there's a chance that the spin wasn't caused by mind power at all. The real culprit may have been air currents generated by the heat of your hands.

Although air currents can't explain how you made the spin stop or reverse itself, you should follow Ken Batcheldor's example and gradually introduce stricter controls. See if you can still spin the device without putting your hands near it. If you can, try putting it inside a transparent box and testing to find out whether your influence still works.

Whether or not you test positive for PK, you can still try a levitation experiment, provided you can find two friends to help you.

One of you sits on an upright chair. The others stand one on each side, facing each other. To make explanations easier, I'll call your seated friend 'the Victim'.

The standing people each place two fingers underneath the Victim's arm and knee. When the fingers are in place, they should try to lift the Victim off the chair. Chances are they won't be able to.

Now the person on the right places her right hand on the Victim's head, palm down. The person on the left then places his right hand, palm down, on top of it. The first person then adds her left hand, then the second person adds his, so all four hands make a little tower.

They should then press down firmly on the Victim's head while chanting, 'Lift... lift... lift...' in unison. Continue the pressure and chanting for at least one full minute, then, on a signal, they should *very quickly* put two fingers back under the Victim's arms and knees and lift directly upwards. Done properly, stopping the chant, releasing the pressure, inserting the fingers and lifting should all be part of a single, fluid process.

Done properly, the Victim will shoot up in the air to shoulder height.

Take great care not to drop him.

12
Divination by Runes

According to an ancient Nordic saga,* one poor woman fell ill and almost died because someone placed inappropriate runes, carved on whalebone, in her bed. Although the runes that haunted Europe's Teutonic history are an archaic alphabet, they've always had a fearsome reputation for their magical powers. Wizards employed them to write spells or lay curses. But by far their most common use was divination: humanity's age-old attempt to get some help about the future.

There were twenty-four original runes, traditionally divided into three equal sets, each of which was dedicated to a Norse god – Freya, Hagal or Tiw. This is what they looked like:

FREYA'S EIGHT   ᚠ ᚢ ᚦ ᚨ ᚱ ᚲ ᚷ ᚹ

* *Egil's Saga.*

HAGAL'S EIGHT ᚺᛁᛁᛃᛁᛚᚲᛃᛊ

TIW'S EIGHT ᛏᛒᛗᛖᛚᛟᛞᛜ

If you're interested in divination – and who isn't? – a good way to start is by making your own rune-stones.

Collect twenty-five flat, light-coloured pebbles of much the same size. Paint the symbols shown above on twenty-four of them, leaving the last one blank. To make sure your runes will give you years of service, apply a coat of clear varnish when the paint has dried. This seals the stones and protects the symbols. Then buy or make a small drawstring bag to keep them in.

Home-made rune-stones like this were by far the most common type of divination kit in the ancient Northlands, but you can, if you wish, make your set from wood or leather, although I wouldn't really advise the traditional method of curing the leather in human blood.

You can read the runes in a variety of ways. By far the simplest is known as the Odin's Rune method.

You draw a single rune stone at random from the bag as an indicator of your overall situation.

This can be a lot more useful than it sounds. You might, for example, draw it first thing in the morning to find out the influences on your day. Or you could draw it in answer to a query in the hope it will give you a breakthrough insight.

Probably the oldest method (mentioned by the Roman historian Tacitus, who was born in AD 56) is the Three Rune Spread, in one of its two variations. Decide which variation you're going to use in advance, then draw out three rune-stones, laying them down in a row from right to left. In one variation, the first rune represents your current situation, the second the action you should take about it and the third the new situation that's likely to arise if you do. In the second variation, the first rune represents you at this present time, the second the challenge you face and the third the best outcome you can reasonably hope for.

For a fuller reading, imagine a clock face on the table in front of you. Place the blank rune-stone in the middle to represent your destiny, then place the remainder of the runes, face down in twos, at the points where the numbers are on the clock. Start at twelve noon and go round clockwise.

When all the stones are in place, begin at the one o'clock position, turn over both stones and

The Meanings of the Runes

Rune	Name	Letter	Meaning
ᚡ	fehu	F	**Cattle**, possessions, food, nourishment
ᚢ	uruz	U	**Wild ox**, strength, manhood
ᚦ	purisaz	P	**Thorn**, gateway, giant, demon
ᚨ	ansuz	A	**God**, signals, messenger, trickster
ᚱ	raido	R	**Riding**, journey, reunion, communication
ᚲ	kaunaz	K	**Torch flame**, protection, opening
ᚷ	gebo	G	**Gift**, partnership
ᚹ	wunjo	W	**Joy**, light, happiness
ᚺ	hagalaz	H	**Natural forces**, disruption, hail, sleet
ᚾ	naupiz	N	**Necessity**, constraint, lessons, hardship
ᛁ	isa	I	**Ice**, standstill, frost
ᛃ	jera	J	**One year**, harvest, bounty
ᛇ	eihwaz	E	**Hunting God**, yew tree, defence
ᛈ	perp	P	**A secret**, initiation, uncertainty
ᛉ	algiz	Z	**Elk**, protection, defence
ᛋ	sowelu	S	**Sun**, wholeness
ᛏ	teiwaz	T	**God Tiw**, warrior, victory, guidance
ᛒ	berkana	B	**Birch twig**, growth, fertility, new life
ᛖ	ehwaz	E	**Horse**, movement, journey
ᛗ	mannaz	M	**Man**, self, humanity
ᛚ	laguz	L	**Water**, flow, fluidity, sea, fertility
ᛝ	inguz	NG	**God Ing**, fertility, hero
ᛟ	opila	O	**Inheritance**, separation, home, native land
ᛞ	dagaz	D	**Light**, breakthrough, prosperity, fruitfulness

read them as a pair. Continue the process round the clock until you finish at the noon position. At each position, the two runes must always be read as a pair, one modifying the other. Imagine each pair is a chapter in the story of your future.

The table opposite is your guide to the runes, beginning with the oldest known meanings, highlighted in bold type. In each case I've given you just three or four keywords. If you want more, there are endless books you can buy with extensive explanations, but I wouldn't recommend them. All they really do is present their author's personal take on the basic meanings. You'll do a lot better working this out for yourself.

Using the keywords allows your intuition to come into play. It also gives you a far deeper insight into the workings of the runes. For the very best results, you might even decide to confine yourself to the oldest-known meaning and try to work things out from there.

Start with *fehu*. The oldest known meaning here is 'cattle'. Not very promising on its own, but put it into context. Ask yourself what cattle meant to the ancient Norse. A man who owned a large herd of cattle was rich in that community. He was known as having many *possessions*. In the wider context, cattle meant *food* for the clan. Food is, of course, physical *nourishment*, a term that might be taken symbolically to include the spiritual *nourishment* you get from religious practice or perhaps just a beautiful sunset.

Tackle *uruz* the same way. Historically, the ox has been used as a beast or burden, but only the domestic ox. The *wild ox* was far too big and strong for anybody to try to put it to work. You met one, you ran. The thing positively embodied *strength*. In the macho environment of the Norse tribes, strength was far and away the greatest qualification for *manhood*.*

Work your way through the rest of the list, checking your conclusions against the additional keywords given. If they disagree, try to figure out why.

* In one modern source I noticed this rune was also interpreted as 'womanhood' in a nod to political correctness. You can make up your own mind whether the ancient Norse would have agreed.

Some of the runes are trickier than others so you may need to do a bit of research. How do you get from the God Ing to fertility, for example? Simple enough: Ing was the god of fertility. Why would a Hunting God be associated with a yew tree and defence? Yew is the best wood for the bow used in hunting... and that bow kept your enemy at a distance in times of war.

Put in the work and the runes will start to make sense. If you get something wrong, don't beat yourself up. It's a closely guarded secret of wizardry that *any* meaning you attach to an oracle will work *provided you believe in it*. Admittedly, it will work rather better if it's the same meaning lots of other people attach (because of something a scientific wizard named Rupert Sheldrake has called *morphic resonance*) but you can go a long way with your own beliefs so long as you stick to them and don't chop and change.

This principle holds good not only for runes, but for a whole host of other divination systems. For thousands of years, wizards have attempted to divine the future in a wide variety of ways. In prehistoric China, they heated the shoulder-bone of an ox and interpreted the marks when it cracked. In Sumer they studied the flight of birds.

In Ancient Rome, they examined the entrails of a slaughtered animal. Long before you were born, they even scrutinised the patterns made by tea leaves when you'd finished drinking, but the invention of the tea bag has put paid to that.

Despite all this activity, you may be surprised to learn sensible wizards never use these systems to predict the future. Nearly 2,000 years ago, the mysterious author of the *Chaldean Oracles* – the last sacred book of classical antiquity – put the situation very bluntly:*

Direct not thy mind to the vast surfaces of the Earth [divination by making marks on the ground] *for the plant of truth grows not upon the ground. Nor measure the motions of the Sun* [sun sign astrology] *collecting rules, for he is carried by the eternal will of the Father and not for your sake alone. Dismiss from your mind the impetuous course of the Moon* [moon magic] *for she moveth always by the power of necessity. The progression of the stars was not generated for your sake* [astrology again]. *The wild aerial flights of birds* [used for divination in classical Greece and Rome] *give no true knowledge, nor the dissection of the entrails of victims* [another ancient practice]. *They are all mere toys, the basis of mercenary fraud. Flee from these if you*

* With my own explanations of what he was talking about in brackets.

would enter the sacred paradise of piety where virtue, wisdom and equity are assembled.

But if wizards aren't predicting the future with these systems, what are they doing? Several things really:

1. They are examining the full potential of their current situation.
2. They are seeking insights into likely outcomes.
3. They are finding guidance on what actions they should take, what choices they should make.

The point is, wizards don't believe the future is somewhere out there, set and fixed, just waiting for us to reach it. They think we make it as we go along. So every worthwhile system of divination is a way of examining *today*, not tomorrow.

13
The Dangers of Magic

Several hundred years ago – in 1458 to be exact – a Jewish wizard by the name of Abra-Melin was facing a dilemma. His son Lamech showed every sign of an interest in wizardry and was clearly the person who should inherit his father's magical knowledge.

But tradition was against it. Lamech was Abra-Melin's *younger* son and in those days, Jewish wizards only ever passed on magic to their eldest.

The magic in question was Cabbala (now more often spelt Qabalah), a centuries-old mystical system that's still, by and large, the foundation of almost all Western wizardry today. The secrets of Cabbala were supposed to have been whispered to Adam in the Garden of Eden by the Archangel Gabriel and thence passed 'mouth to ear'* from father to first-born son.

* Which is what *Cabbala* literally means.

There was no way Abra-Melin could possibly break such a hallowed chain, however much he wanted to.

Then he had an inspiration. Why not leave the Cabbalistic secrets to his eldest boy, Joseph, exactly as tradition dictated, but pass on another, quite different, magical system to the enthusiastic Lamech? Fortunately Abra-Melin had access to just such a system. It had been passed down to him by his father, Simon. Abra-Melin had tested the system for himself and confirmed that it worked perfectly. It was the ideal gift for Lamech.

Abra-Melin hurried to write down everything he could remember about the system, placed the text in a casket and handed it with his blessing to his younger son.

Wizards know all about this obscure little piece of family history because a French translation of Abra-Melin's book found its way into the *Bibliothèque de l'Arsenal*, a major library in Paris that was established in 1797. Exactly a century later, it was rediscovered by a British wizard named MacGregor Mathers, who translated it into English.

The magical methods contained in the book are fascinating. Cabbalistic magic centres on a peculiar diagram called the Tree of Life, which is used as a focus for meditation and visualisation. Simon's system – now usually referred to as the Abra-Melin system – was very different. It begins with a hugely complicated ritual that can only be started at Easter and takes six months to complete.

During the whole of this time, the would-be wizard has to wake every day before dawn and pray in an oratory which he has set up specially and dedicated to the purpose. The text explains:

Having carefully washed one's whole body and having put on fresh clothing: precisely a quarter of an hour before Sunrise ye shall enter into your Oratory, open the window and place yourselves upon your knees before the Altar, turning your faces towards the window; and devoutly and with boldness ye shall invoke the Name of the Lord, thanking Him for all the grace which He hath given and granted unto you from your infancy until now; then with humility shall ye humble yourselves unto Him and confess unto Him entirely all your sins; supplicating Him to be willing to pardon you and remit them...

More prayers have to be offered each day at sunset.

From the outset you are required to abstain completely from sex and alcohol, eat a specific diet and conduct your business with scrupulous fairness. Later, your obligations towards the ritual become even more onerous until eventually you have to give up any other occupation, cut off contact with the outside world and dedicate yourself to it completely.

The purpose of the whole elaborate rite is to obtain the 'knowledge and conversation' or your Holy Guardian Angel, an immensely powerful superhuman – and supernatural – entity who will henceforth be your guide and spiritual teacher.

But the magic of Abra-Melin doesn't end there. In fact, the knowledge and conversation of the Guardian Angel is only the beginning. More than half of the Abra-Melin text is devoted to information on a whole host of spirits – both good and bad – along with instructions on how they can be called up and controlled by means of *magic squares*.

This is what a magic square looks like:

S	A	T	O	R
A	R	E	P	O
T	E	N	E	T
O	P	E	R	A
R	O	T	A	S

In fact the SATOR formula is perhaps the most famous of all magic squares. It turned up scrawled on a wall of a Roman villa near Cirencester, in Britain. It has been found inscribed on old bibles and drinking vessels and seems to have been seen as a protection. But it's not one of the Abra-Melin squares, which I don't want to reproduce here for reasons that will be obvious a little later.

In the Abra-Melin system, each square was linked to a spirit and had a specific use, like revealing the location of a gold mine or helping the magician fly in the air. Abra-Melin warned his son most fiercely that the squares should never be used until he had successfully achieved the knowledge and conversation of his Guardian Angel. Without the angel's protection, they were far too dangerous.

Although there are some scholarly reservations about the *Book of the Sacred Magic of Abra-Melin the Mage* – the French text appears to date to the eighteenth century and there's little indication it was translated from Hebrew – MacGregor Mathers claimed the magic squares seemed to have a power all their own and would 'fascinate small animals' if left lying around.

But while most wizards have at least heard about the book, very few have made use of the system, almost certainly because of the need to dedicate six months to a difficult ritual before you can safely expect results. The dark wizard Aleister Crowley attempted the whole operation in a remote house on the shores of Lough Ness in Scotland and unleashed a horde of nasty spirits which some believe haunt the area to this day. More recently, a London wizard managed the full six-month rite in a basement flat and wrote a book about his experiences.* Annoyingly, he stopped short of spelling out what happened when his Guardian Angel was supposed to appear.

The temptation has always been to cut to the chase and see what would happen if you simply used the magic squares without bothering your Holy Guardian Angel. That way, you save yourself six months hard work and grab all the benefits right away. One European wizard – I'll call him Daniel – did exactly that. What happened to him is instructive.

Daniel began very cautiously. He had a lot of respect for the Abra-Melin system and his expectation was that it would bring results. But without angelic protection, he wanted to make sure he knew what he was dealing with. Some of

* *Sacred Magician, a Ceremonial Diary*, by Georges Chevalier, Paladin, London, 1976.

the spirits listed by Abra-Melin sounded suspiciously like devils. One was named as Beelzebub, the notorious Lord of the Flies in Hebrew mythology.

So instead of rushing in, he called on a psychic he knew to watch while he drew up an experimental magic square. He picked one associated with what seemed to be a fairly harmless spirit and aimed at promoting friendship – a result unlikely to do any harm to anybody.

When he completed the square, the psychic reported that something was standing behind him. The good news was it didn't seem to be a devil. The bad news was it didn't seem to be a spirit either. In fact she'd never seen anything quite like it in her life. It was a living entity in the shape of a funnel. It was twisted as if looking over Daniel's left shoulder.

A few more experimental squares later, the psychical investigation showed that each time one was drawn, weird three-dimensional living shapes appeared, but nothing particularly threatening. Daniel thanked the psychic and decided he could safely use the Abra-Melin squares without the need for the six-month ritual.

At first things went rather well. Daniel found himself in court facing property charges serious enough to earn him a prison sentence if he was convicted. His main problem was he had no defence – he was, in fact, guilty. So instead of wasting his money on a lawyer, he decided instead to create a magic square 'to obtain the favour of a judge'. Fifteen minutes after his case was called, he was freed on a legal technicality.

Greatly encouraged by this result, Daniel began to experiment with the squares more often. Some of the results he obtained were unexpected. When, for example, he drew up the square that promised to aid a man to fly through the air, nothing seemed to happen... until a friend presented him with a plane ticket. Locating a gold mine was just as interesting. Within minutes of drawing the square he picked up a magazine that contained an article on gold mining in South Africa. The locations of several mines were mentioned, none of which, of course, was of any practical use to Daniel.

It seemed to him that the Abra-Melin magic was working, but not always in a predictable way. All the same, his experience in court encouraged him to continue and he managed to achieve some further small successes.

But then things started to go wrong.

At first they were small – little disasters that could happen to anybody. His car broke down, leaving him stranded on a remote country road with a mobile phone that was out of credit. (And nothing with which to write an Abra-Melin square.) Some children broke a window of his house, then rain blew in and destroyed important paperwork. His dog fell ill and while the animal recovered, the vet's bill was enormous.

Daniel didn't connect any of these incidents with his work on the Abra-Melin system. But he was already learning to be very cautious from other experiences with the squares. The problem was, Abra-Melin wasn't always entirely clear about what you might expect from a particular square. One promised to 'cast a spell upon the liver' without saying what the outcome of this might be.

Several squares were supposed to compel the spirits to bring various things. He wrote one for timber, which he needed for a shed he was building. Miraculously a small load of timber appeared in his back yard overnight, but it had been dumped there by thieves who had stolen it from a nearby building site. Daniel was subsequently questioned by the police and narrowly missed being charged with receiving stolen goods.

The real rot set in when he wrote squares that promised visions. To aid the process, he began taking drugs. From that point, his life ran like a Victorian morality play. The drug use led to addiction, which cost him both his job and his wife. He ended up hospitalised with a nervous breakdown.

It seemed a heavy price to pay for ignoring Abra-Melin's safety instructions.

14
Creating a
Soul-Stone

Sometimes, of course, the magic you need isn't as complicated as Abra-Melin. It's not so much a case of wanting something specific, such as to curry favour with a judge or to win £20 at bingo; it's more about needing something that will make things better generally, perk up your luck and smooth your path in life.

In those circumstances, wizards recommend a talisman.

A talisman is an object small enough to carry with you or to wear, like a ring or a pendant or a piece of crystal. It works a bit like a battery. But instead of storing electricity, it stores magic.

You can buy talismans all over the Internet, but before you part with your money, you'd be well advised to remember there are only three types of talisman that actually work:

1. A talisman made by a wizard who knows what he or she is doing. (Which rules out all

the mass-produced junk and some handcrafted items.)

2. A talisman made personally for you by a wizard who knows what he or she is doing. (Which is always better than No. 1.)

3. A talisman you make for yourself. (Which, if you happen to know what you're doing, is usually better than Nos. 1 or 2.)

Wizards believe, as you may have gathered by now, that magic works from the inside out; and that holds good whether a talisman is made for you or you make your own. But when a talisman is made for you, the wizard creates a magical energy inside himself which is then passed into the talisman and eventually works to change you on the inside. When you make one for yourself, the process of making it changes you to begin with and the energy you put into it *feeds back* to increase results.

The very oldest form of talisman – and the most effective – is a soul-stone. It's particularly easy to make. Here's how:

Take yourself out for a walk and keep your eyes open for a suitable pebble. The only two things you need to remember are that it has to be small enough for you to carry comfortably and that it must *feel right*.

Feeling right is important. Wizards say it's not

so much a question of you picking a stone as the stone picking you. You have to be relaxed and patient, free from any preconceptions. Given time, a suitable pebble will jump out at you.* Clean it off and bring it home.

Then paint it.

Take time deciding how. What you're creating here has to be taken seriously. In many ways it's like choosing your mystery name. You need to find colours and a design that reflect your essence. The stone will be a representation of what you are inside.

Many of the soul-stones I've seen use abstract patterns, but some have little pictures of animals or human figures. Shamanic power animals turn up quite often. There's no right or wrong in this. It's your stone and it will be right – that's to say it will have power – in direct proportion to the effort you put into making it.

When the painting is finished, you might think of sealing it with a clear varnish. Alternatively, keep it in a small pouch. Either way the painting is protected. Keep your soul-stone with you and note the effect it has on your life.

* Metaphorically speaking.

Soul-stones are wonderful talismans, but there may come a time when you'll find it useful to store a particular sort of arcane energy. This creates a much more *focused* talisman, one that can be used to specific effect.

Have a look at the table below, which gives the planets and their associations. Decide what type of talisman you want to make. If you need something to help with your love life, then you'll make a talisman of Venus. If you're looking for an improvement in your health, then create a talisman of the Sun. If you want to communicate more effectively, a talisman of Mercury will help. And so on.

Your next step is to check which metal goes with your chosen planet:

PLANET	METAL
Sun	Gold
Mercury	Liquid mercury
Venus	Copper
Moon	Silver
Mars	Iron
Jupiter	Tin
Saturn	Lead

The tricky one here is Mercury. The associated metal is both liquid and toxic. While you *can* use liquid mercury to create a talisman, I wouldn't

		SUNDAY	MONDAY	TUESDAY
PLANETARY HOUR AFTER SUNRISE	1st	Sun	Moon	Mars
	2nd	Venus	Saturn	Sun
	3rd	Mercury	Jupiter	Venus
	4th	Moon	Mars	Mercury
	5th	Saturn	Sun	Moon
	6th	Jupiter	Venus	Saturn
	7th	Mars	Mercury	Jupiter
	8th	Sun	Moon	Mars
	9th	Venus	Saturn	Sun
	10th	Mercury	Jupiter	Venus
	11th	Moon	Mars	Mercury
	12th	Saturn	Sun	Moon
	13th	Jupiter	Venus	Saturn
	14th	Mars	Mercury	Jupiter
	15th	Sun	Moon	Mars
	16th	Venus	Saturn	Sun
	17th	Mercury	Jupiter	Venus
	18th	Moon	Mars	Mercury
	19th	Saturn	Sun	Moon
	20th	Jupiter	Venus	Saturn
	21st	Mars	Mercury	Jupiter

advise it until you're an experienced wizard. So for the moment, let me explain how you use the other metals and we'll come back to Mercury later.

Before working on your talisman, you need to know the best time to make it, which involves calculating something called the *planetary hour*. Find out the times for sunrise and sunset on the day you've set aside to make your talisman. (This information appears in a surprisingly large number of newspapers, usually along with the weather forecast.) Work out the amount of time between the two and divide by twelve. The answer is the length

WEDNESDAY	THURSDAY	FRIDAY	SATURDAY
Mercury	Jupiter	Venus	Saturn
Moon	Mars	Mercury	Jupiter
Saturn	Sun	Moon	Mars
Jupiter	Venus	Saturn	Sun
Mars	Mercury	Jupiter	Venus
Sun	Moon	Mars	Mercury
Venus	Saturn	Sun	Moon
Mercury	Jupiter	Venus	Saturn
Moon	Mars	Mercury	Jupiter
Saturn	Sun	Moon	Mars
Jupiter	Venus	Saturn	Sun
Mars	Mercury	Jupiter	Venus
Sun	Moon	Mars	Mercury
Venus	Saturn	Sun	Moon
Mercury	Jupiter	Venus	Saturn
Moon	Mars	Mercury	Jupiter
Saturn	Sun	Moon	Mars
Jupiter	Venus	Saturn	Sun
Mars	Mercury	Jupiter	Venus
Sun	Moon	Mars	Mercury
Venus	Saturn	Sun	Moon

of the planetary 'hour' for the date in question.

Once you know the length of the planetary hour, you can work out your best starting time from the table above:

Let's suppose you want to make a Jupiter talisman on a date when the planetary hour is fifty minutes long. Let's also suppose the date happens to fall on a Wednesday. Looking down the Wednesday column, you'll find Jupiter listed opposite the 4th, 11th, and 18th planetary hours. That gives you three possible starting times: 200 minutes (three hours, twenty minutes) after sunrise,

550 minutes (nine hours, ten minutes) after sunrise or 900 minutes (fifteen hours) after sunrise.

Ideally, you should complete the work during the planetary hour you started with, but if that's not possible, come back to it in another planetary hour associated with your metal.

After all that, you'll be pleased to hear the work itself is fairly simple. Take a small sheet of the metal you'll be using, not more than two inches square.* On one side engrave or paint the relevant planetary *sigil*, or magical symbol, from the following table:

PLANET	SIGIL	PLANET	SIGIL
SUN		MERCURY	
MOON		VENUS	
MARS		JUPITER	
SATURN			

* If you find gold or silver financially taxing, you can use gold or silver coloured foil on a thin wood or card backing.

If you're really, really weak at drawing, you can use the relevant planetary square in place of the sigil, taken from this table:

SUN

6	32	3	34	35	1
7	11	27	28	8	30
19	14	16	15	23	24
18	20	22	21	17	13
25	29	10	9	26	12
36	5	33	4	2	31

MERCURY

8	18	59	9	64	62	63	1
49	15	14	52	53	11	10	56
41	23	22	44	45	19	12	48
32	34	35	29	28	38	39	25
40	26	27	37	36	30	31	33
17	47	4	20	21	43	42	24
9	55	54	12	13	51	50	16
64	2	3	61	60	6	7	57

MOON

37	78	29	70	21	62	13	54	5
6	38	79	30	71	22	63	14	46
47	7	39	80	31	72	23	55	15
16	48	8	40	81	32	64	24	56
57	17	49	9	41	73	33	65	25
26	58	18	50	1	42	74	34	66
67	27	59	10	51	2	43	75	35
36	68	19	60	11	52	3	44	76
77	28	69	20	61	12	53	4	45

VENUS

22	47	16	41	10	35	4
5	13	48	17	42	11	29
30	6	24	49	18	36	12
13	31	7	25	43	19	37
38	14	32	1	26	44	20
21	39	8	33	2	27	45
46	15	40	9	34	3	28

MARS

11	24	7	20	3
4	12	25	8	16
17	5	13	21	9
10	18	1	14	22
23	6	19	2	15

JUPITER

4	14	15	1
9	7	6	12
5	11	10	8
16	2	3	13

SATURN

6	1	8
7	5	3
2	9	4

While these might seem worryingly similar to the Abra-Melin squares mentioned in an earlier chapter, they can be used quite safely since they have very different associations.

For the special case of Mercury, you'll need to make or buy a small linen or leather pouch. Paint the square or sigil on that, then fill it with a mixture of dried lavender, parsley and oat – all plants associated with Mercury. Sew the pouch closed.

Later in this book you'll find out how to charge your talisman to make it more effective, but even now it will automatically attract the proper energies and feed them to you while you have it in your pocket.

15
Astral
Doorways

In March 1994, a small group of black-robed wizards met privately in a darkened room in Lancashire to engage in a bizarre experiment. Soberly, silently, they took their seats in a circle around a single, lighted candle. There was an air of expectancy in the room… and some tension. The goal of the experiment was to put the group in psychic contact with Atlantis.*

Like most wizards, the Lancashire group believed our world is reflected in the Astral Light[†] and hoped some astral ruins of Atlantis might remain. They planned to spot them using something called an *astral doorway*. The term *astral doorway* is used by wizards to describe any technique (or in some cases a piece of special equipment) that produces astral visions.

* For a full examination of the Atlantis legend, see Herbie Brennan's *Forbidden Truths: Atlantis and Other Lost Civilizations*, Faber and Faber, London, 2006.
† See pp. 238–48.

But what they were attempting here was new magic, an astral doorway never used before. It had been created by one of their number, a wizard who specialised in astral work. No one knew what to expect. The problem was, most astral doorways produce different visions when used by different people. With a whole group involved, there might be chaos.

In fact, the experiment was a complete success. Miraculously, the wizards achieved a single vision. They were able to 'see' the same things at the same time and confirm details to one another.

A week later, a second group of wizards operating in London attempted to duplicate the experiment. They too managed a single vision... of a sea voyage that agreed with the Northern group in a whole host of areas:

1. Both groups felt a strong connection with the Atlantean priesthood, rather as if they were reaching back through time. Both groups felt welcome in the Atlantis they visited.

2. Individual members of each suggested the experiment was only a start, that the contact should be maintained and further work done. Members of both reported the feeling that their group had somehow been 'selected' for the work and reported feeling 'privileged'

that they were permitted to take part.

3. Both groups felt there was a two-way process involved. They had the idea that the Atlanteans wanted something from them.

4. Both groups experienced their ship as having a crew and being fully supplied. Both groups saw their craft as having a high prow. The Northern group was agreed that their boat was of reed construction.

5. Although both agreed Atlantis was in the Atlantic Ocean, each took a different route. Both, however, managed to end up in exactly the same place, although they approached it from different angles.

6. Both groups reported lower sea levels than we have today. Both groups mentioned islands in the Atlantic leading in a chain to Atlantis. Both groups were led by dolphins.

7. All participants experienced themselves as dressed the same way. Men and women both wore an Egyptian kilt and little else. The London group mentioned that some Atlantean men were also dressed this way.

8. Both parties were met by a small gathering of people when they landed on Atlantis. Both groups experienced Atlantis as having tropical flora. Both groups saw and entered a white building, which proved to be a temple.

9. Both groups mentioned a labyrinth inside the temple and described its floor plan as circular with an inlaid tiled floor. Both groups said the building was aligned to certain stars. Both groups began to chant in exactly the same way at the conclusion of their experiments.

Following the success of the two experiments, the wizard who'd created the astral doorway released details of his new technique for use by wizards everywhere. If you can put together a group of six or more, you can use it yourself. If you can't, you might even adapt it to solo use and trigger an interesting journey in your imagination.

For group work, you need a darkened room, a circle of chairs and about twenty minutes for a warm-up exercise that can be carried out anywhere you won't be disturbed. Start the exercise by breaking the working group into pairs. One from each pair becomes Member A, the second Member B.

Member A starts by picking a familiar room in her home. This could be a living room, bedroom, dining room, or even a garden shed. The important thing is that it must be an *actual* room, not somewhere she's made up. Member A is going to clean it – mentally.

Ask Member A to decide what equipment she wants for the job. Everything's available – buckets, sprays, detergents, soap, stepladders... you name it. Member A then starts to visualise cleaning the room and tells Member B, *in detail*, exactly how it's being done.

The room should be cleaned in the following sequence:

1. Start with the ceiling and clean it, then go down the walls.
2. As you reach pictures, bookcases etc., clean them and move them so you can clean behind them.
3. Clean individual items such as books, ornaments as you reach them.
4. Clean the furniture and, if necessary, move it into the centre of the room so you can reach any surfaces behind it.
5. When ceiling, walls, furnishings and ornaments have all been cleaned, clean the carpet then lift the carpet and clean the floor underneath.

As you clean, decide which items you're going to keep and which you're going to throw out. Store items for throwing away just outside the door. Small items go in a packing case, larger items can just be piled up in a heap.

When the cleaning's finished, double check

what you want to throw out and what you want to keep. Then go outside and either burn the rubbish in an imaginary bonfire, or dump it in an imaginary lake.

Throughout the whole thing, it's important that Member A describes what's going on in the greatest possible detail, right down to mentioning the colour of ornaments, the titles of books, what scenes are shown in pictures and so on.

When Member A is done, it's Member B's turn. The exercise finishes when Member B has cleaned his room as well.* The group can then enter the darkened room for its visit to Atlantis.

Before the experiment starts, you need to elect a Lore Master and a Seer. The Lore Master is the person who reads out the story that sets the scene for the experiment. The Seer's job is a bit more complicated. She – it's often a woman – starts things off when the story is finished by telling the group how she imagines the journey continues and invites them to join in as the pictures start to form in their minds. If, at any time, the group as a whole can't agree on what they're looking at in their mind's eye, then the Seer's version should be taken as official.

You need to explain that neither the Lore Master nor Seer are in any way leaders of the

* A side-effect of this exercise is that it stimulates unusually vivid dreams.

group. The whole point is that everyone takes part. Each and every person present should say what they see and join in discussions and decisions. Don't let anybody take charge.

Once everybody gains confidence, the group will tend to function more and more strongly as a team.

To start the experiment, dim the lights. Place a single candle or night light in the centre of the room as a focus for the group which sits in a circle around it. When everyone is comfortable, the Lore Master should read aloud the following story – technically known as a *pathworking* – in a low, soothing voice:

We will start by following in the footsteps of the ancient Greek philosopher Solon, whose records gave Plato the oldest story we have of Atlantis. We are going to the Temple of Sais on the Nile Delta in Egypt, more than two thousand years ago. There the priests will allow us access to the timeline of Atlantis. Sit upright and relax as completely as you can. Breathe regularly and slowly, relax a little more then close your eyes.

To begin the working, listen and imagine…

We stand among the Priests of Sais before the House of Amen in the Southern Harim, that same Egyptian temple visited so long ago by Solon. The great pylons of the Temple tower on either side of us, their host of flag-

staves fluttering in a veritable cornfield of brightly coloured pennons. Your eyes trace the huge reliefs of Pharaoh, rampant and heroic as a bull, smiting down his enemies with an upraised mace.

You look away from the reliefs and back to the flag-staves. They are of wood from Lebanon, like the massive entrance door between the pylons. Thutmose, Father of the God, moves a pace; and so they all move, a dignified procession towards the door. Sekhet, on the left of Thutmose, reaches out with that large left hand of his to take the ceremonial staff and knock once on the door. The sound reverberates dully. Then, as he steps back a pace, the door swings open and we are faced by the night priests.

The Father of the God among the night priests steps forward to present Thutmose with a papyrus scroll, an inventory of Temple contents and effects.

'Is all correct?'

'My Brother, all is correct.'

The night priests walk into the sunlight. We pass with the day priests into an open courtyard surrounded by a colonnaded porch. This porch is new, its columns commissioned by the Pharaoh as a gift to the Temple, carved and brightly coloured to represent the lotus flower. We move from the courtyard down three shallow steps into the hyperstyle, a transverse, columned hall lit only dimly by its clerestory windows. Here the priestesses await us.

The High Priest Khaemuas inclines his head in greeting to the Chief Priestess and she bows briefly back. The priestesses move to take their places among the priests, humming softly to the accompaniment of the little hand sistras they carry. The group now walks slowly to the sanctuary, the single chamber in which stands the god's own shrine.

Like the hyperstyle, the room is dimly lit, but eyes soon adjust so that the heroic frescos on the walls are clearly discerned. The scenes depicted are all of the Pharaoh: the Pharaoh at war, the Pharaoh triumphant, but most of all, the Pharaoh engaged in the great observances of his religion.

189

The stone shrine of the god is enclosed by two folding wooden doors, fastened with bolts and papyrus strings, sealed with a large clay seal.

A priest steps forward and begins to kindle the censer, a well-formed metal arm, the hand of which holds an incense pot. As the smoke began to curl upwards, he hands it to the high priest who censes him, the company, the sanctuary and finally himself. The sweet, heady scent of incense drifts through the chamber.

Khaemuas, the High Priest, sets down the censer and reaches out to break the papyrus string and seal which secures the door bolts to the shrine.

'The twin doors of the sky are opened!' he recites. 'The two doors of the earth are unclosed. Geb gives greetings, saying to the gods who abide upon their seats: Heaven is opened! The company of gods shines forth! Amen-Ra, Lord of Karnak, is exalted upon his great seat! The Great Nine are exalted upon their seats! Their beauties are thine, O Amen-Ra, Lord of Karnak!'

Within the shrine is a single crystal.

'Purified, purified is Amen-Ra, Lord of Karnak!' Khaemuas proclaims and pours a stream of purest water into the crystal. 'Take to thee the water which is in the eye of Horus; given to thee is thine eye, given to thee is thy head, given to thee are thy bones, established for thee is thy head upon thy bones in the presence of Geb!' The water streams from the image and is absorbed in the sand.

Open your eyes now and look directly into the candle flame. Allow yourself to become receptive to the crystal energies.

Once you feel the link forming – and it shouldn't take very long – close your eyes again, visualise the crystal on the shrine as clearly as you can, then mentally ask it to open up an area of its structure so you can enter its inner form. Don't feel shy about this. Whatever orthodox science may believe, crystals can be thought of as living forms, possibly even intelligences.

The crystal in the shrine will open a doorway of light. See it in your mind's eye and enter through it into the inner structure of the crystal. Take a moment to familiarise yourself with it, look around you, feel the walls, then search for the pathway established by the ancient priests. You will know when you find it, for it is like a stream, the same stream of pure water Khaemuas poured on the great crystal just moments ago. Follow the stream until you emerge in the Athens of long, long, long ago...

This part of the pathworking leads directly into the group experience itself. Participants are asked quietly to open their eyes and the Lore Master then sets the scene with the following words:

This working starts in Athens, sometime prior to 10,000 BC.

Conventional wisdom suggests a primitive culture just beginning to develop agriculture, but we will use a wizard knowledge gained from different sources. According to the most ancient of Egyptian records, the city state of Athens existed at that time and was, in fact, a powerful political force.

The Ice Age, which hindered the evolution of civilisation in Northern Europe and the British Isles, had left the Mediterranean virtually untouched, although the mean temperature was certainly lower than it is today. This would have influenced cultural development, injecting a note of dynamism lacking in a hotter climate.

For the working, we are about to make a sea journey to Atlantis. Athens, our starting point, is inland, as you know, but there are indications of ancient roads to the harbours of Phalerum, Munychia, Zea, and Kantharos.

At this point, the Lore Master breaks off to ask the group for its first decision – which road they will take. Whichever is chosen, he should describe in a few words of his own what happens when they take that road. The Phalerum road went direct to Phalerum harbour. Munychia, Zea, and Kantharos harbours were approached via the walled settlement of Piraeus.

When they reach the harbour, the Lore Master tells his colleagues they are boarding a sailing ship, *but leaves it to the group* to describe the ship itself, how they board it and so on. This has the effect of encouraging the group to use their visual imagination before the voyage actually starts.

Once everyone is safely boarded, the Lore Master describes the beginning of the voyage using the following pathworking fragment:

The ship moves away from harbour and soon you are sailing through the Saronic Gulf. If you look to the north, you can see the island of Salamis. Southward that island is Aegina. But we are sailing westward before we turn south to join what will one day become the Roman corn supply route from Alexandria in Egypt to Ostia and Rome itself.

In following this route we cut between Sicily and the toe of Italy, then follow the Sicilian coast westward before venturing again into deep water. This will take us south of Sardinia, along the northern coast of Africa and, eventually, through the famed Pillars of Hercules (now the Straits of Gibraltar) into the Atlantic Ocean.

At this point, the Lore Master tells the group they have another choice to make. The original account of Atlantis (published by Plato) did not specify its exact location. One source placed it due south, off the west coast of Africa. Another claimed it lies to the west, but far closer.

The group is then asked to decide on the direction they wish to sail.

From this point on, the Lore Master stops describing what is happening and invites the Seer and the other members to take over.

The voyage proper has begun.

16
Remembering Past Lives

Imad Elawar lived in the Lebanon, in a very remote, somewhat primitive village – one of those places where time stands still and people don't travel very far from the place where they were born.

But though he hadn't travelled far, Imad one day started to claim he'd lived before as somebody called Ibrahim Bouhamzy in a village called Khriby about thirty kilometres from Imad's home. He went on and on about this to anybody who'd listen until he had his family bored stiff with the whole affair.

Then one day Imad bumped into somebody he recognised from his past life, a man who actually came from Khriby. When they questioned the visitor, Imad's family discovered he had been a neighbour of... Ibrahim Bouhamzy.

This astonishing coincidence gave them the

incentive to investigate. They quickly discovered something very strange was going on. When questioned, Imad produced no fewer than forty-seven pieces of information about the Bouhamzy family – detailed information with names and places. He even mentioned that as Ibrahim Bouhamzy he'd an affair with a woman called Jamile. When they checked, they discovered that forty-four of the forty-seven were absolutely accurate.* How did Imad, in a little isolated Lebanese village, know so much about what was going on in a family thirty kilometres away? You might say that he picked up the information from friends, or read about it in the local paper, or maybe even slipped over for a quick visit to Khriby when nobody was looking. You might say all of that, quite reasonably, but you'd be wrong. When Imad Elawar started talking about the Bouhamzys and his mistress Jamile, he was only two years old.

Case histories like this – and there are scores of them all over the world – have convinced many wizards that reincarnation is a fact of life. You don't go to heaven or hell when you die. You're reborn in a brand new body to live life all over again as somebody else. But wizards go further. They claim to have discovered

* The remaining three couldn't be proven.

techniques that will actually allow you to remember who – or what* – you were in your past lives.

One of the strangest is a method known as the *Christos Technique*, which is widely credited in magical circles to an Australian wizard, although there is some indication it may have originally been developed in America.

Experimenting with the Christos Technique requires three people: the person who will remember the past life and two helpers. Here's how it works:

1. Begin by having your subject lie flat on his back on the floor. Put a small cushion or pillow under his head so his neck is straight

* One American wizard investigating a past life discovered he'd been a gorilla.

and he can lie comfortably. Have him remove his shoes. Socks, stockings or tights may be left on. In this position, the subject closes his eyes.

2. Have a helper begin gently to massage the subject's ankles. A light, circular motion on the ankle bones is what is required here. Until you experience it, you'll find it difficult to imagine how relaxing this is.

3. After about a minute and while the ankle massage is still going on, place the edge of your curved hand on the subject's forehead so that it rests between the eyes, fitting snugly into the hollow at the root of the nose. In this position, it covers the traditional site of the legendary Third Eye of Oriental Yoga, equated in the West to the pineal gland. Once your hand is in position and with the ankle massage continuing, begin a vigorous circular rubbing movement which should be continued until your subject reports that his head is buzzing. Make sure he remains fully relaxed. If tension has crept in, have him take several deep breaths and go limp.

That's all there is to the physical aspect of the method, although some wizards let the ankle massage continue gently throughout the rest of the session since it helps the subject to stay relaxed. Should it prove distracting, you can always stop it at a later stage.

The mental aspect of the method now begins. The sequence goes like this:

1. Instruct your subject to keep his eyes shut and visualise his feet. He should try to make this (and all the following visualisations) as vivid as possible, so long as the effort doesn't spoil his relaxation. Remember your subject isn't in trance. He can talk to you as much as he likes without messing things up. So…

2. Have him tell you when he's managed to visualise his feet successfully, then instruct him to imagine himself growing two inches (about five centimetres) longer through the soles of his feet. He should try to feel the sensation of growing and see the result in his mind's eye.

3. Wait until the subject tells you he has managed Stage 2, then instruct him to return to his usual length. He should try to imagine the sight and feel of his feet returning towards him to their normal position.

4. Repeat this process at least three times – more if necessary – until your subject gets used to it and can visualise the 'growth' really easily. Don't hurry this: it's an important

part of the method and one that lays the foundation of much that follows. Wait each time until your subject tells you he's been successful. Your patience at this point will be rewarded later.

5. Now repeat the whole thing, but this time ask your subject to grow through the top of his head then return to his normal size. If you've taken the time to run him properly through the foot business, this should be fairly easy. Once again, repeat it at least three times.

6. Return your subject's attention to his feet and this time ask him to 'grow' out twelve inches (thirty centimetres) then return to his normal length. Make certain he's done this successfully before moving on.

7. Repeat the twelve-inch growth and shrinkage through the top of the head.

8. Return your attention to the feet and ask your subject to grow out twenty-four inches (sixty centimetres). Interestingly enough, you'll discover that the fact someone can successfully make a mental two inch stretch doesn't automatically guarantee he'll be able to go further. Have him keep trying until he manages the twenty-four-inch stretch (which he should manage in under a minute) but this time *do not* have him return to normal size.

9. While your subject feels he is still stretched twenty-four inches through the soles of his feet, have him *simultaneously* stretch twenty-four inches through the top of his head. Weird though it sounds, some subjects find that as they start to stretch through their heads, their extended feet begin to withdraw. Have him keep trying until he gets the two-way stretch and here again do *not* have him return to normal size.

10. While at full stretch through head and feet, ask your subject to expand all over, as if he was blowing up like a balloon. Keep him trying until he can feel himself extended beyond the limits of his physical body. Most of us think of swelling as uncomfortable, but in this instance the sensation is very pleasant.

11. At this stage your subject is, so to speak, out of his body. He should still be reasonably relaxed. (Although maybe a little excited.) You should now move on to the next stage by asking him to visualise and describe his own front door. Get him to do this in great detail. Ask him the colour, the number of panels, the name on the lock. Push him for as much information as you can.

12. Next, ask him to imagine he's standing on the roof of his home and have him describe

what his garden and immediate surroundings look like. Here again, you should ask as many questions as necessary to satisfy yourself that he is mentally viewing the scene in detail.

13. Now comes a tricky bit. Have your subject imagine he's levitating straight up in the air until he's floating above his home at a height of 1,500 feet. This sort of height is meaningless to most people so don't get too fussy about it. What you're after is really just to have him see things from *way up* above his home.

14. Once your subject is hovering at 1,500 feet, have him mentally turn around in a complete circle, all the time describing what he can see. Encourage him to turn slowly and, as before, ask questions. You want to know what the landscape looks like from this height, what landmarks he can see, what activity, if any, is taking place on the ground.

15. Ask what time of day it is.

16. If your subject has been describing a day scene, ask him to change it to night-time and tell you what he sees. (If the original scene was at night, ask him to change it to daytime.) When he's done that, ask him to change it back again and compare the two scenes.

17. Ask who's changing the scene from day to

night and back again. Your subject may be puzzled by the question, but the whole point of it is to get him to see that *he* is the one making the changes. Remind him that this shows he has complete control over what he's experiencing. Assure him he'll stay in control throughout.

18. This is the really interesting part. Once you're sure your subject is entirely comfortable with his new imaginary viewpoint, have him shoot up still higher until he loses sight of the ground below. Have him change the picture to bright sunshine (if that is not what he already sees) then have him come back down to earth and land feet first.

If all's gone well, he'll land in a past life.

17
The Odd Art of Crystal Gazing

The first British spy to be given the code-name 007 wasn't James Bond. He was John Dee and he worked in the Secret Service set up by Sir Francis Walsingham for Queen Elizabeth I in 1569.

But Dee wasn't just a spy. He was a wizard with a library of arcane lore that numbered some 4,000 books – the largest of its type in England. He spent years engaged in crystal gazing.

You probably think of crystal gazing as fairground fortune-telling. Wizards take it a bit more seriously. John Dee took it very seriously indeed. He believed it could put him in contact with angels.

The trouble was, for all his wizardry, Dr Dee couldn't make a crystal work for him. He knew the ceremonies that were supposed to call up angels, but never knew if they worked. If angels came, he couldn't see or hear them. This wasn't unusual for wizards and Dee did what wizards have always done in such circumstances – he hired a psychic to do his crystal-gazing for him.

In fact he hired two, but the first one didn't last long. The second, engaged at a salary of £50 a year, was an Irish scoundrel named Edward Kelley. They began their experiments in 1582 and carried them on for five years despite various unconnected adventures.

A flavour of what they got up to is neatly caught in this extract from an unusual account published by Meric Casaubon in 1659 and entitled *A True & faithful RELATION of what passed for many Yeers Between Dr JOHN DEE (A Mathematician of Great Fame in Q. Eliz. and King James their Reignes) and SOME SPIRITS*:

Suddenly there seemed to come out of my Oratory a Spirituall creature, *like a pretty* girle *of 7 or 9 yeares of age, attired on her head with her hair rowled up before and hanging down very long behind, with a gown of Sey... and seemed to go in and out behind my books... and as she should ever go between them, the books seemed to give place sufficiently...*

DEE   *I said... Whose maiden are you?*
SHE   *Whose man are you?*
DEE   *I am a servant of God both by my bound duty and also (I hope) by his Adoption.*
A VOYCE   *You shall be beaten if you tell.*

SHE   *Am not I a fine Maiden? Give me leave to play in your house, my Mother told me she would come and dwell here.*

DEE   *She went up and down with most lively gestures of a young girle, playing by her selfe, and diverse times another spake to her from the corner of my study by a great Perspective-glasse, but none was seen beside her self.*

SHE   *... Shall I? I will. (Now she seemed to answer one in the foresaid* Corner *of the Study.)... I pray you let me tarry a little (speaking to one in the foresaid* Corner*).*

DEE   *Tell me who you are.*

SHE	*... I pray you let me play with you a little and I will tell you who I am*
DEE	*In the name of Jesus then tell me.*
SHE	*... I rejoyce in the name of Jesus and I am a poor little* Maiden, *Madini, I am the last but one of my Mother's children, I have little Baby-children at home.*
DEE	*Where is your home?*
MA	*I dare not tell you where I dwell. I shall be beaten.*
DEE	*You shall not be beaten for telling the truth to them that love the truth, to the eternal truth all Creatures must be obedient.*

Dee was, of course, communicating with Madini second-hand. It was Kelley who spoke for the girl, or allowed the girl to speak through him like a Spiritualist medium. By June 1583, the two men believed themselves to be in contact with an impatient angel called Ave, who dictated a series of Calls or evocations to the 'Watchtowers of the Universe,' which were claimed to make up the system of magic known as Enochian, already mentioned briefly in this book.

The way Dee and Kelley took down the Calls was bizarre. They'd somehow obtained, or created, more than a hundred large squares, which they called tablets, measuring about 49 x 49 inches, each filled by a grid pattern of letters. During the course of the experiments, Dee would place the tablets in front of him on a writing table, while Kelley would sit across the room staring into a crystal shewstone that now rests in the British Museum.

When contact was made, Kelley would report sight of the angel in the shewstone, along with the angel's own copies of the tablets. Using a wand, the angel would then point to certain letters on the tablets. Kelley would call out their rank and file. Dee would then locate the letter in the same position on his tablet and write it down. Because the Calls were so powerful, the angel dictated them not only letter by letter but *backwards*, so that each had to be reversed before it could actually be used.

Before he had met Dee, Kelley had had his ears cropped for coining.* He lived on his wits and was involved in extracting money from several innocent investors on the pretence that he could turn lead into gold. He died in 1597 while trying to escape from jail. In these

* You don't hear of coining any more. But in the days when coins were made from real gold and silver instead of the rubbish they use nowadays, you could shave a little off the edge of each one and so build up a nice little collection of precious metal.

circumstances you might suspect he made up his talk of angels to keep Dee happy and hold on to his £50 a year.

The problem with this is that the Enochian calls are not a code or cypher, but an actual language. It's just possible Kelley invented it, for artificial languages have certainly been created: Esperanto is a modern example. But it would have required huge time and effort. Furthermore, Kelley would then have had to memorise the Calls – there are forty-eight of them – so perfectly that he was able to dictate them backwards, letter by letter. Given Kelley's dislike of honest work, it's almost easier to believe he really did talk to angels.

But whatever about that, many wizards have since reported interesting results from this sort of work. Technically, what Dee and Kelley did is called *scrying* or sometimes *scrying in the spirit vision*. It can be carried out using concave mirrors or obsidian lenses, but the most popular tool remains a polished sphere of rock crystal. Magicians believe rock crystal (clear quartz) is almost unique in that its structure is exactly the same on both the physical and astral levels. Because of this, it makes a fabulous astral doorway.

Some of the more effective scrying techniques

involve going into trance – a dangerous procedure as I can personally attest. But fortunately there are other methods.

Your first task will be to find yourself a crystal sphere. It has to be quartz crystal. Lead crystal or glass won't do. The bad news is that genuine polished crystal spheres are expensive. The good news is you don't need a big one. The enormous *crystal ball* (usually moulded glass) of the fairground is show business, not wizardry. I've seen good results from a crystal sphere that isn't much larger than a marble.

You can usually find a selection of polished spheres in any store that sells quartz crystals generally. Pick the one you're going to use intuitively. Take your time, relax and let one draw you towards it. In this way it's like your soul stone: let the crystal choose you. Don't worry if the sphere isn't perfectly clear. In fact, small flaws and imperfections in the heart of the crystal will help it function better for scrying.

When you take it home, hold it under running water for a few minutes to clean off any subtle energies it may have picked up in the shop. Then prepare yourself for scrying with this special crystal meditation:

Begin by sitting legs uncrossed, spine straight, in an upright chair. Hold your crystal sphere cupped in one or both hands and take a few minutes to examine it properly. Look for any rainbows that arise from the way it reflects light. Turn it round and pay attention to the small flaws inside it. Let yourself get really familiar with the crystal so you'd know it again if it was stored in a box with a hundred other spheres.

Once you feel you know your crystal well, relax your body, hold your crystal in your lap and close your eyes.

In a reflection of the Atlantis experiment described earlier, mentally ask your crystal to open a pathway you may use to enter into its perfect form. When it does so, imagine yourself following the pathway into the heart of the crystal. Take time to explore the inner structure, which may present itself as a crystalline cavern, or a vast chamber or some other form entirely. This is not an experience you can get from books. Every crystal is unique, as is the way it presents itself. It is possible you will hear sounds with your inner ear, even feel different temperatures or textures.

The first few times you use the technique, look on it as a simple exploration and come back out again after a maximum of about ten minutes. Once you're happy that you're familiar with the inner structure of your crystal sphere and can enter it with ease in a wholly relaxed state, you're ready to begin scrying.

There are two methods you can use, neither of which involves trance.

The first is tricky and frankly doesn't work for everyone. But when it *does* work, the visions in the crystal are quite extraordinary. There is nothing vague about them. They appear with the clarity of a photograph or movie and seem completely real.

Begin by relaxing as deeply as possible and allowing your mind to drift. Hold the crystal sphere in your lap and gaze into it without any particular effort. Now cast your mind back to those novelty Magic Eye pictures you may have seen which appear to be a jumble of coloured dots until you look at them in the right way. At that point, they suddenly turn into a 3-D image.*

Allow your eyes to unfocus slightly, exactly as you would do to view the novelty pictures. Stay relaxed, with your mind still drifting. With luck and perhaps a developing skill, a strong image may appear abruptly in the crystal. If you stay relaxed, you should be able to hold the picture. Any degree of tension will dismiss it at once.

* If you haven't seen pictures of this type, go to www.magiceye.com. They're also available as novelty books and posters. Take the time to track them down in your area and practice until you get the hang of seeing the 3-D image.

The second option, easier but less spectacular in its results, is to use your crystal sphere as an astral doorway. Enter into it imaginatively as you did for the preliminary exercise, but this time when you're inside, look for an exit on, so to speak, the 'other side' of the crystal.

Leaving by this exit will take you into an imaginal landscape where scrying visions will arise spontaneously.

18

How to Leave Your Body... and Live!

Something very strange may be about to happen to you. It's possible – although you're not going to believe it – that you could wake up one day and discover you've turned into a ghost. You'll find you can do all the things that ghosts are supposed to do, like walk through solid walls and float up into the air. You can creep up on someone and say *Boo!* although you'll find they won't be able to hear you. They won't be able to see you either, come to that. You'll be quite invisible to everyone... except another ghost.

Nobody else will tell you this, but according to some very intensive research, there's a one-in-four chance of that happening to you at least once during your lifetime. That's another way of saying if you're part of a family of four – mum, dad, sister, brother – one of you is going to float off sometime. Perhaps more to the point, it's *most likely* to happen in your teens, while your hormones are still playing up.

Very few people talk about this sort of thing. You probably won't talk about it either. But if it happens to you, you need to know...

* You aren't dead.
* You aren't about to die.
* You aren't ill.
* You aren't nuts.
* You're not in any danger.
* You *will* be able to get back into your physical body.

The phenomenon is known as an Out of Body Experience, or OOBE for short. But wizards call it something else – astral projection. They believe you can be trained to do it whenever the fancy takes you.

Wizard training for astral projection is based on the curious idea that you have two bodies.* One is the physical body you're using to hold this book. The other is an astral body, which is in every way a mirror image of the physical, but made from far finer material – perhaps even just energy. For most of your life, your astral body coincides exactly with your physical; is locked into it, in fact. But sometimes, as the result of

* Actually most wizards believe you have more than two, but I don't want to complicate things.

puberty, an accident, certain drugs (notably hospital anaesthetic), deep relaxation, trance, natural causes or wizard training, it can get shaken loose.

Here are some of the exercises wizards use:

Exercise One
This exercise, like the one that follows, is designed as preliminary training. It won't trigger a full-scale projection, but if you do it properly it will make you feel quite odd (in a nice sort of way).

You can do it indoors or out. All you need is a clear space.

1.   Stand with your feet slightly apart, your arms hanging at your sides. Make sure you're nicely balanced and relaxed. Keep your eyes open. As you stand in this position, sense your body at rest. Become aware of how it feels. After a moment...

2.   Slowly raise your right arm. Feel the sensations associated with the movement. Concentrate on these sensations and try to remember them. Lower your arm slowly. Repeat the arm raising several times, concentrating on the sensations of the movement each time. Now...

3.   *Imagine* you are raising your right arm.

Imagine as vividly as you can all the sensations associated with lifting it, but leave your physical arm by your side. Wizards call this *raising your astral arm*. I'll use this term for the process throughout the remainder of the exercise. Remember, when I instruct you to raise or lower your astral arm, you are to imagine all the sensations of the movement while keeping your physical arm still. Now lower your astral arm.

4. Raise and lower your physical right arm.
5. Raise and lower your astral right arm.
6. Alternate raising your physical and astral right arms twice more.
7. Repeat steps 1. to 6. with your left arm. Pause for a moment, then...
8. Roll your physical shoulders forward and concentrate on the sensations of moving them.
9. Roll your astral shoulders in exactly the same way. That's to say, imagine vividly the sensations of rolling your shoulders, while keeping your physical shoulders still.
10. Alternate between rolling your physical and astral shoulders forward two more times. Then...
11. Roll your physical shoulders backwards.
12. Roll your astral shoulders backwards.

13. Alternate between physical and astral shoulders two more times. Pause, standing relaxed with your arms by your sides, then...

14. Make a (physical) fencing lunge to your right. That's to say, you should step forward with your right foot, lean your body to follow it and extend your right arm as if you were thrusting with a sword in your hand.

15. Return to the upright position with your arm by your side, then repeat the lunge physically.

16. Make an astral fencing lunge to your right.

17. Alternate between physical and astral lunges to your right two more times.

18. Make a physical fencing lunge to your left. Return to the upright position.

19. Repeat.

20. Make an astral lunge to your left.

21. Alternate between physical and astral lunges to your left two more times.

22. Physically lunge to your left, return to the upright position then lunge right. Return to the upright position.

23. Make an astral lunge to your left, then return to centre.

24. Repeat.

25. Make an astral lunge to your right, then return to centre.

26. Repeat.
27. Make a physical lunge to your right, return to centre, and immediately make a lunge to your left. Return to centre.
28. Make an astral lunge to your right, return to centre, and immediately make an astral lunge to your left. Return to centre.
29. Now send your astral body lunging to the right while your physical body lunges to the left. Return to the centre.
30. Send your astral body left and your physica body simultaneously right. Return to the centre.
31. Alternate sending the bodies in opposite directions several times.
32. Spin slowly in both directions first physically, then astrally.
33. Jump in the air first physically, then astrally.
This concludes the exercise, but you may if you wish try starting a movement – any movement – physically, then carrying it on astrally.

With that little bit of fun under your belt, you can go on to the next preliminary exercise:

Exercise 2
1. Set up a chair before a full-length mirror. Sit in the chair, relax and study yourself in the mirror *not* as if you were looking at a reflection, but rather as if you were actually

seeing yourself from the outside. Try to imagine it's the *real* you in the mirror.

2. Scrutinise yourself *in detail*, trying to discover things about yourself that you never noticed before. Imagine you were meeting yourself for the first time... and were required to write such a detailed description that it could be used to identify you in a Court of Law.

3. Stand up, directly in front of the mirror, and stare directly into your reflected eyes. Hold your own eyes until you begin to feel unsteady and start to sway.

4. Sit down again and once more look into your reflected eyes. Begin to repeat your own name over and over, aloud, in a monotone. This will make you feel peculiar after a time. Reinforce the feeling by strongly imagining that your real self is that reflection in the mirror; that, in other words, the essential you is *out there*.

Although not designed to trigger a projection, those two exercises can sometimes be all you need, if you happen to be somebody likely to project naturally. It's unlikely to happen unless you're totally relaxed, but it's as well to be aware of the possibility.

Many wizards, however, prefer to use a controlled form of projection, known technically as the *Body of Light*, which brings them most of the benefits of a full projection, but isn't as scary. This is how they do it:

Find a comfortable chair in a room where you won't be disturbed. Relax, using any method you find works for you.

Now imagine you're no longer seated in your chair, but standing in the room about six feet away. Try to visualise yourself as clearly as you can. Make a real effort to paint in *detail*... Try to 'see' what you are wearing. Imagine the scuff marks on your shoes. Count the buttons on your jacket. Note the way your hair falls over one eye. Examine the expression on your face. Visualise in colour and in depth.

Spend as much time as you need to build up this imaginary figure fully. A good idea is to set aside a particular time each day for the exercise and devote ten to fifteen minutes daily to it for a week or more.

In the next stage of the exercise, imagine you're rising from your chair and walking around the room. Close your eyes and try it. Remember how the room looked from your chair and visualise it. If you find the details difficult, open your eyes again for a refresher. Keep working at it until you can describe the room in detail with your eyes closed.

Next, imagine yourself rising from your chair and walking slowly round the edges of the room in a clockwise direction. Try to see in your mind's eye how the perspective of the room changes as you move. Try to remember any small objects or ornaments that aren't visible from your chair.

If you have difficulty with this part of the exercise, open your eyes, stand up *physically* and walk around the room. Then sit down, close your eyes again, and try to duplicate the journey in your imagination. Keep working on it until your visualisation becomes easy and vivid.

Now try the same walk *anticlockwise*.

Once all this comes easily, stay put physically,

but try visualising yourself in *another* room, again walking around it first clockwise, then anticlockwise. When you've thoroughly explored the second room, mentally extend your range and visualise yourself wandering through your entire house.

The next step is to imagine yourself exploring some more distant, less familiar scene. Indoors is easier for most people, but if you are feeling really confident, you might try imagining yourself outside.

Now comes the crunch. If you've followed instructions, you've trained yourself to do two things. One is to visualise a mirror image of yourself standing a little distance from where you're seated in your chair. The other is to imagine yourself walking around various locations and examining them in detail. The final step is to combine the two.

First, visualise the mirror image. Do this with your eyes open if at all possible. When the figure is definitely there, *imagine yourself looking out from its eyes*. Imagine the room from the viewpoint of the figure you have created. Look around and note the details, including your own (physical) body seated in the chair. Once you feel you're firmly seated in this imaginary body, have it walk around the room in a clockwise direction, exactly as you did in the earlier part of the exercise. You should find this fairly easy, but if not, just keep trying.

If you practise the exercise over several days, one of two things will happen. Either you'll gradually find you can 'see' vividly from the new body, or you'll reach a point where suddenly the imagined body seems more real to you. Either way, you get back to your physical body by *reversing* the initial process. From the viewpoint of your new body, simply visualise how the room looks from the physical body sitting on the chair. (Actually returning to the physical is seldom a problem. Most wizards find the real difficulty is staying in the imaginary body they've created.)

At this point, you have to be asking yourself whether you're *really* out of the body when you do the exercise. Test it out by exploring somewhere you've never been before in your imaginary Body of Light, then go visit the same place physically. And try not to be *too* shocked if you discover that the scene you saw while in your imaginary body is confirmed in every detail when you visit the spot in reality...

19
Wizard Dreaming

You may not think you dreamed last night, but you'd be wrong. Everybody dreams every night, barring high fever, insomnia and certain drugs. You may not think you dreamed in colour last night, but you'd be wrong about that too.

But you don't dream at the same rate throughout your life. As a baby, you dreamed about half your sleeping time. When you grew up, this dropped to between a quarter and a fifth. If you live past sixty-five, there'll be a slight increase in your dreaming time, although you won't go back to a baby's dream pattern whatever they say about second childhood.

The reason why so many people think they never dream at all is that dreams are easily forgotten. And while dreams actually occur in colour, they often fade to black and white when you do remember them.

Some scientists think dream activity is caused

by random stimulation of one part of the brain by another. (Your dreams are just you trying make sense of these random stimulations during sleep.) Others say it's your mind's attempts to bring new experiences into line with older, stored memories. Still others have come to the conclusion that dreams are just your brain trying to rid itself of bad, accidental connections between its cells and you'd be far better off not remembering them.

Wizards are convinced all these theories are rubbish. Some of them think dreams are sent by the gods, and can be used to predict the future, devise medical cures and receive information. Others look on them as gateways to different levels of reality. All of them take dreams very seriously indeed.

There was a time when nearly everybody did the same. In the Old Testament you'll find how a great famine in Egypt is revealed in a dream of the Pharaoh, as interpreted by Joseph. In the New Testament, Pilate's wife advises her husband to have nothing to do with the conviction of Christ because of a dream.

Historical sources show that the Roman Consul's wife, Cecilia Metella, convinced the Senate it should rebuild a temple to Juno Sospita because of a dream she had. The Emperor

Marcian dreamed he saw the bow of Attila the Hun break... on the same night Attila died. Plutarch records how the Emperor Augustus decided to leave his tent after a dream, even though he was ill at the time. A few hours later, his bed was pierced by enemy swords. The wealthy King Croesus accurately saw his son killed in a dream. Calpurnia tried to warn her husband Julius Caesar about his impending assassination because of a dream.

Another Roman, the writer Cicero, records how a traveller dreamed his friend needed help. He awoke, thought it over, but decided not to take the dream seriously and went back to sleep. He promptly dreamed about his friend again. This time the man claimed he'd been murdered and his body hidden in a cart. Both the cart and the body were later found.

The trouble with this sort of thing is you can never be sure when dreams are predictive and when they're just caused by worry, or something you saw on television. Which is why a whole tribe of wizards worked out a better way to make use of them.

The Senoi are a native people found on the Malay Peninsula and the coastal plains of Eastern Sumatra. There are about 18,000 of them alive today and just about every one –

men, women and a sizeable proportion of the children – practises wizardry.

Although the Senoi are, on the face of it, a fairly primitive lot – they still live mainly as hunter-gatherers using blow-guns and poisoned darts – their reputation as wizards is so strong that neighbouring tribes have been afraid to attack them for generations. As a result, they've largely forgotten what war is like. But that's not all. They've been free from violent crime and mental illness for the past two centuries.

They've managed this by means of wizard dreaming.

The system was brought to them by their own full-time wizards, known as *Tohats*, who got it from spirit guides during their shamanic trance journeys. Every morning, every Senoi family sits down to share a breakfast and its dreams. Children are encouraged to describe their previous night's dreams which are then explained to them by their elders, who give tips for better dreaming. Family sessions are followed by daily tribal councils, where the dreams of the adults and older children are discussed and examined.

In a typical session, a youngster might complain she'd had a nightmare about falling. Her excited family would tell her at once this was about as good

a dream as you could get. She'd be asked to supply more details – where she fell to, what she found when she got there – and reassured there was nothing to worry about. The dream simply meant the falling spirits loved her and were trying to call her into their spirit world. If she simply relaxed and let go of her fear, she could meet them in a future dream.

The emphasis is always on freedom from fear. Even if you die in a dream – the worst nightmare of all – the Senoi will tell you it just means you're receiving power from the spirit world. After a few sessions like this, Senoi youngsters stop dreaming they're falling and start dreaming they're flying.

The aim of the system is to get complete mastery over the spirit (dream) world, something believed to bring huge benefits in the physical realm as well. If this type of wizardry appeals to you, the first thing you have to do is catch your dreams.

This isn't easy. Although you have several dreams each night, the chances are you'll remember only one or two a week. Worse still, the only dream you're likely to remember is the last one you had just before waking in the morning. Even then, it's typically gone in a few seconds. You *might* remember an earlier dream if you happened to wake up in the middle of the night, but here again it pops like a soap bubble.

The only answer to the problem is self-training.

Start by leaving a notebook or tape recorder by your bedside. When you go to bed, tell yourself firmly that you *will* remember all your dreams. When you wake up, either during the night or in the morning, write down or record your dreams *at once*.

Those last two words are critical. The day you're tempted to turn over and catch another forty winks is the day you lose your dream. Even *thinking* about something else can drive the dream away. Wake up, write down, don't wait. That takes real willpower, but it's the only way. Don't try to make sense of what you remember: record it with all its peculiarities intact.

To begin with, you should write down every detail of the dream you can remember. Later you can just take notes and write them up during the morning. If you simply can't remember your dream despite all your efforts, you can sometimes trigger your memory by returning to the sleeping position you were in when you awoke. Another useful trick is to try to capture the overall feel of your dream, rather than the details. Ask yourself, *Was the dream pleasant or unpleasant? Did it take place in the city or in the country? Did any of my friends appear? Was there a particular theme? What was the overall shape?*

The good news is that with practice, remembering gets easier. But remembering is only the first step. You can only turn yourself into a dream wizard by applying the Senoi system. Fortunately the basis of the system is very simple indeed. It boils down to just three points. In your dreams you must always...

1. Confront and conquer danger. This turns dream enemies into friends. Always move

towards danger and fight if necessary. Recognise that the power of your enemies is *your* power which they've stolen from you. So the more powerful your enemy, the more powerful you are. When you defeat an enemy, *demand* a gift to bring back in the form of a song or a poem or a piece of useful information. If attacked by friends, remember they are really spirits wearing your friend's face like a mask in order to confuse you. But if it happens, make an effort in waking life to renew your friendship so the spirit can't damage your relationship.

2. Advance towards pleasure. Don't worry about forbidden relationships as your dream lover is simply wearing a reassuring and familiar mask. *Request* the gift of a song or poem afterwards to represent the love and pleasure between you.

3. Achieve a positive result. If you find yourself falling, try flying. Find out where the spirits want you to go. Explore the new environment and take careful note of it. Keep a lookout for anything that would be of value in your waking life.

The Senoi believe that anyone – with a little help from their friends – can outface, overcome and eventually make good use of everything that turns up in the dream universe. They know from experience that goodwill shown towards others during your waking hours will ensure their help in dreams.

One great way your friends can help you is to learn the Senoi principles themselves, so you can all share your dreams.

20
The Inner Castle

'It's possible', said a teacher at one of Britain's most respected Schools of Wizardry, 'to work magic in a cupboard.' She paused, then added as an afterthought, 'It's even possible to work magic in a shoebox.'

She was commenting on the concerns of a pupil who complained he hadn't the money to build a magical Lodge room or temple.

A typical magical temple in the Western Esoteric Tradition – twin pillars, double-cube altar, magus throne in the east, chequerboard tiled floor – is indeed expensive to set up. But as the teacher said, you can set up miniature equivalents of the furnishings in a broom cupboard, or even a shoebox. The reason why they still work is that magic doesn't depend on place, it depends on what's going on inside your head. If your little model helps you *visualise* a full-scale temple, then you're up and running as a wizard.

Inner buildings like this are commonplace in wizardry, but few are more useful than the Inner Castle.

The construction of the Inner Castle is usually taught as a *pathworking*, which you'll recall, is a guided meditation. Many magical schools create special castles for specific purposes. In one, for example, the Inner Castle is an analogue of the human body and pupils learn how to use its chambers to control their physical functions and promote self-healing.

But more interesting – and in some ways more useful – is the discovery that many (perhaps all) of us carry an Inner Castle *already built* in the depths of our unconscious minds. Occasionally you can be guided to it by inner helpers – one student was carried to hers on the back of a white horse during a meditation reverie – but most wizards use specific techniques. Here again, the most usual is a pathworking, but this time instead of spelling out the details of the castle's structure, the pathworking only leads you to it.

To be effective, the pathworking must tap into certain mythic elements already present in the wizard's mind. The nature of these elements is generally a matter of upbringing. In other words, a pathworking that leads a Tibetan Buddhist to his Inner Castle wouldn't be expected to work for an Australian Aborigine.

The following brief working is based on what wizards call *The Matter of Britain,* the cycle of myths and legends associated with King Arthur and his Knights of the Round Table. As such, it will prove effective for students brought up in the British Isles, North America, Germany, France, Denmark, Norway, Sweden, Poland and Hungary.* Record the words for playback or have a friend read them to you when you are in a relaxed state. Allow the images to arise strongly in your mind's eye.

You are standing outside, in the British countryside, but a countryside remote in time where there are no sounds of cars or planes to break the silence.

Behind you is a simple cottage, perched near the summit of a low hill. Before you is a rough stony track that curls away behind the hill to disappear from sight. Follow that track now.

At first the path takes you through cultivated fields, then woodland, but soon you find yourself walking through a lonely marsh so that you may no longer leave the track.

The marsh is eerie, desolate and remote, as if gripped

* The list isn't exhaustive. If you live outside these countries, it's still worth trying. The Matter of Britain has a surprisingly broad appeal.

by an enchantment, but you persevere and finally emerge on to a fertile plain. In the distance, outlined against the skyline, is the silhouette of a castle, moated and silent.

As you come closer, you can see pennants flying from its turrets and you note that the path you are on leads directly to the main entrance where a drawbridge has been lowered as if in welcome.

Although there don't seem to be any people about, the castle looks well cared for and as you approach you are struck by a sudden realisation. This is your *castle, your property, your stronghold, awaiting your return...*

From this point, you're on your own. Cross the drawbridge to enter your castle, take time to explore and keep a careful written record of what you find.

Some of it may surprise you.

21
Evidence
of the Divine

The first words of the first chapter of the first book I ever wrote were an obscure, difficult quotation. It went like this:

The composite form of the sphinx also represents by hieroglyphical analogy the four properties of the universal agent, that is to say the Astral Light – dissolving, coagulating, heating and cooling. These four properties, directed by the will of man, can modify all phases of Nature, producing life or death, health or disease, love or hatred, wealth even or poverty, in accordance with the given impulsion.

The quote comes from a very old work called *The History of Magic.* It was written during the nineteenth century by a French deacon of the Roman Catholic Church named Alphonse Louis Constant. Since he was nervous of showing a public interest in wizardry, he used the pen name

'Eliphas Levi'. Most of the book is easy reading, but I found that paragraph bewildering.

The sphinx was fine. Everybody knows about the sphinx. It's a gigantic statue that crouches in the sands of Egypt a short walk from the pyramids. I could even understand why he said it was a 'composite form'. The sphinx has the body of an animal – most people think it's a lion – but the head is that of a man. Furthermore, the head is too small for the body, as if it was an afterthought.

With a little bit of work, I figured out 'hieroglyphical analogy' as well. Hieroglyphs are the ancient picture-writing of Egypt. Some of their symbols stand for alphabet letters, but others stand for whole words. When you want to write OWL in Ancient Egyptian, for example, all you need is a little drawing of an owl: 🦉

I knew a lot of wizards believed the design of the sphinx hid magical secrets in symbolic form. Maybe Levi's 'hieroglyphical analogy' was just a fancy way of saying it. *Hieroglyphical* because hieroglyphs were used in Egypt. *Analogy* because that's the way symbols work.

But after that I crashed. What was an 'Astral Light'? How could it be a universal agent if I'd never heard of it? Above all, how could directing its properties produce life or death, wealth or poverty, disease or health? It sounded as if Levi (who had no mean reputation as a wizard) was spelling out some huge, powerful magical secret and I hadn't a clue what he was talking about.

I started to read up everything I could about the Astral Light. It turned out there wasn't much. What there was proved very, very old and just as difficult to understand. But several modern wizards did write about the Astral *Plane* and I thought that might be the same thing. The trouble was, it didn't sound like the same thing. Nobody was talking about Levi's 'universal agent' or anything remotely like it. They were talking about a *place*.

The Astral Plane sounded like another level of reality. The wizards seemed to think it was a spirit world. Ghosts lived there; and strange, disembodied intelligences. Some of them were positively fairy tale – sylphs, gnomes, salamanders and things like that. You could visit it yourself by means of something called *astral projection*.

Which was all very interesting, but it got me no closer to understanding Levi. It seemed clear that even if you managed to find the mysterious Astral Plane, there was no way you could use it to influence events in *this* world. Nobody was claiming it had anything to do with life or death, poverty or riches. Clearly, the Astral Light and the Astral Plane were not the same thing.

Except they were.

Sometimes the truth isn't out there – it's right under your nose. But that's often the best place to hide it. I struggled for ten years to understand what Levi was talking about. During that time, several wizards told me quite plainly. Yet somehow I couldn't hear them. What they were saying didn't make any sense. What they were saying was that the Astral Plane was all imagination.

Your parents have a lot to answer for. They teach you the way the world is. (Presumably the way their parents taught *them*.) They teach you the sun sets in the west, two and two are four and humans rule the planet. They teach you that what goes on inside your head is just imagination. (Note that word 'just'.) They tell you it's daydreaming, wool-gathering. They make absolutely certain you believe imagination isn't real. They probably convince you it's worthless as well.

But wizards don't believe their parents. Wizards have ideas about imagination that would make your hair curl.

Let's start with Levi's Astral Light.* The

* Yes, I figured it out eventually.

Astral Light *is* imagination. It's not *created* by your imagination. (Or anybody else's.) It's the actual *substance* of imagination. It's the stuff that makes imagination work. As Levi said, it's everywhere – a universal agent. Without it, there would be no pictures inside your head. Without it, you could never dream. Without it, there would be no magic.

Wizards readily admit the Astral Light lies outside the range of your physical senses. Nor has it been detected by any electronic instrument, so far as I know.* But that doesn't mean you're not aware of it. Close your eyes and think of England. You're using the Astral Light.

Walk along a city street in daylight. See the cars, the shops, the people and the buildings. Without the daylight you'd see none of them. Without the daylight there'd be only darkness. Wizards say it's like that on the inner levels. Without Astral Light there would be only darkness behind your eyes. Without Astral Light your imagination would be blind.

Wizards have secretly investigated the Astral

---

* There's a long-running problem about this sort of thing. Scientists don't believe in things like the Astral Light because they can't detect it with their instruments – and won't look for it with their instruments because they don't believe in it. But that may change. Quantum physics is forcing scientists to rethink some of their old prejudices, notably when it comes to universal agents.

Light for centuries. They've made two important discoveries about its nature. The first is that it's an infinitely flexible chameleon. You can mould it into anything you want and it will change colour to suit. The second is that you can shape it *with your mind*.

The implications are enormous. If you want to build yourself a house using bricks and mortar, it's a big deal. Ordinary physical matter is difficult to shape, heavy to lift, costly to join together. Your house will take many months to complete. You'll need help to build it. Chances are you'll have to use machinery.

If you want to build a house using Astral Light, you simply *think* it into existence. It's there, in place, instantly.

There's no limit to the things you can make this way. But they do have one drawback. Although they appear in the blink of an eye, most of them disappear just as quickly. They're like a jerry-built shack that collapses at the first breath of wind. When you withdraw your attention, your creation is absorbed into the background light.

But some things are more permanent. Wizards stress that the Astral Light isn't just inside your head. It's everywhere. Part of its nature is that it reflects physical structures. It takes on an imprint of any physical structures that *endure*.

Let's say you build a shed in your back garden today. The whole operation, including the finished shed, will be reflected in the Astral Light. Should it fall down tomorrow, it will disappear from the Astral Light at once. It's exactly like a reflection in a mirror.

But build the Great Pyramid and after a few centuries that massive structure isn't just reflected in the Astral Light, but actually imprinted there. If you demolish the pyramid and use the stones to build a three-metre high wall around France, the astral imprint will still be

there, stately and in a single piece. It won't stay there forever, but it will last a long time.

Wizards claim something else about the Astral Light. They say it doesn't just reflect the physical world, but other realities as well. Places like the spirit world. Or those parallel universes physicists and sci-fi writers keep talking about. You get imprints from beyond as well.

Now you can understand why the Astral Light really is the same thing as the Astral Plane. But you can also see why the Astral Plane sounds so much like a place. You never really become aware of the Astral Light *in itself.* What you see are things reflected in it. It's like admiring yourself in a mirror. The stunning creature you're looking at is so interesting you forget the mirror itself.

All of us, wizards or not, use the Astral Light each night in order to experience dreams. The dream worlds we 'visit' are part of the Astral Plane. Most of them we create ourselves, unconsciously moulding the Astral Light in accordance with our fantasies and nightmares. But sometimes we stumble on structures that are already there, firmly imprinted on the Light. And sometimes we meet up with living creatures from the worlds beyond.*

* Actually we only meet up with their astral reflections, but it gets tedious spelling this out each time.

Most of us use Astral Light during the day as well. It's the raw material from which we form our fantasies and daydreams. In fact, we're so busy creating fantasies and daydreams we seldom ever experience the Astral Light for what it really is or catch more than a glimpse of the things reflected in it.

Unless, that is, we happen to be wizards.

Wizards are interested, above all, in mind control – their own minds, that is, not yours. Once you take control of your mind, you can stop stirring up the Astral Light with your dreams and fantasies and start seeing what was there before you muddied the water.

This can be very interesting. You might find reflections of alien vistas. You might discover information you never knew. You might meet up with creatures who could help you do the things you want to do. You might even make some interesting friends. The trick is to learn the difference between what you create yourself – empty daydreams, wish-fulfilments – and the things already there.

By the time you get this far, you've gone a long way towards understanding Eliphas Levi's remarks about the Astral Light. But not the whole way.

There's still that passage about producing life

or death, wealth or poverty by manipulating its properties. It's a passage that relates to one of the most important of all magical secrets. Wizards have discovered that not only does our world influence the Astral Light, but the Astral Light can, in certain circumstances, influence our world.

This is a tricky area and one that's caused a lot of grief. The basic idea is simple enough. If you create something in the Astral Light, it has a tendency to turn up in the physical world.

As you've seen, creating something in the Astral Light is very easy. You just visualise and there it is. And you're free to visualise anything you want, from a brand new Merc to passing an examination. If wizards are saying that wishing will make it so – and they are – you'd think we'd all have everything we wanted by now.

But there's a catch – well, three catches really. The first is that you must visualise *precisely and in detail*. Not many people can do that. You need training and practice – lots of practice. A good place to start is the exercises outlined in the chapter on Wizard Training starting on page 25.

The second catch is that you have to energise your visualisation. That means putting *emotion* behind it. Emotion and the Astral Light are linked. It's no use visualising, however vividly, some outcome you don't really care about. You have to want it, powerfully and deeply. If you don't, you have to *make yourself* want it. What you can't do is fake it.

The third catch is you have to open up the channels. Even fully trained wizards miss this one sometimes. The most perfect, emotion-driven visualisation won't make your new Mercedes appear in a puff of smoke. When the magic works, the result arrives through natural channels. You might win the car in a competition, or find it was part of a legacy. You might even be offered a highly paid job that leaves you rich enough to buy it for yourself. Even though the whole thing starts with your manipulation of the Astral Light, the end result will always seem to come about coincidentally.

You can help or hinder that 'coincidence'. Decide what it is you want. Visualise it clearly and precisely. Drive your visualisation with emotion. *Now go out and try to get it by normal, non-magical means.*

That last bit is what I mean by 'opening the channels'. It allows your desire to manifest. If you sit in your room like a baby bird waiting for a worm, you'll be sorely disappointed. That's not using magic. It's hoping for a miracle.

22
Balancing Your Chakras

Wizards think there's more to you than meets the eye.

Apart from the obvious flesh and bone, they're convinced you have a whole hidden energy system that crackles and sparkles (silent and invisible) throughout your natural life. It's the state of this system that determines your health... and can also influence your ability to work effective magic.

The heart of this system is a series of seven spinning centres called *chakras*, a term borrowed from Indian wizards. Each one works to transform universal energy into personal energy which is then circulated through the human energy field, known as the aura. When the circulation is balanced and strong, you feel great.

The whole of your energy system is so far-reaching you'd need several books to explain it all. But very few Western wizards go into it all that deeply. (It's different in the East where manipulating the system forms a more important part of wizardry.) Instead they concentrate on keeping their chakras in a fit and healthy state.

Although invisible, each chakra has a specific location in the physical body. Here's where you'll find them:

CHAKRA LOCATIONS

CHAKRA	INDIAN NAME	LOCATION
Crown	*Sahasrara–padma*	Centred on the crown of the head
Brow	*Ajna*	Centred between the eyebrows
Throat	*Visuddha*	Centred on the throat
Heart	*Anahata*	Centred on the midline at a level with the heart
Solar Plexus	*Manipura*	Centred on the solar plexus itself
Sacrum	*Svadhisthana*	Centred on the body's midline, four finger widths below the navel
Base	*Muladhara*	Centred on the base of the spine / pubic bone

CHAKRA LOCATIONS

You can get very complicated about chakras.
Each one isn't just linked to various bits of you,
like kidneys or stomach or adrenal glands. It also
influences things like your mental state or your

ability to see visions. But as a preparation for wizardry, all you really need to know is that your chakras can be influenced and balanced using a piece of quartz (rock) crystal.

There's hardly a shaman on the face of the planet who doesn't carry a piece of quartz in his medicine bag. You might find a chunk you could use yourself if you live in the right location, but failing that, you can buy quartz crystals in most New Age stores, some health shops and a few hobby shops. Ask for a clear quartz point, unpolished if possible and try not to spend a fortune since a small one will do.

Clean your crystal when you get it home by holding it under running water. Dry it off and you're almost ready to balance your chakras, an experience I guarantee you will thoroughly enjoy.

Find a quiet room, sit comfortably, with your spine straight and your feet flat on the ground. Hold your crystal in your right hand. Close your eyes and allow your breathing to come naturally and easily. Your neck should be long at the back and your chin tucked in slightly so that your head is well supported. Bring your attention to the base of the spine, close your eyes and have a friend slowly read you the following instructions for a chakra balance meditation.* As you work

* Alternatively, you can record the instructions yourself and play them back.

your way through it, touch each chakra in turn with your quartz crystal point.

Starting at the base of the spine, imagine a strong, clear red light, spiralling outwards from your coccyx, filling your pelvis and flowing right down your legs to your feet:

Say to yourself, 'I accept my instinctual nature, that part of me which is purely animal.'

Move on up to your sacrum and imagine orange light filling your lower abdomen, right across your belly:

Say to yourself, 'I accept my emotional nature, my need for pleasure and nurturing.'

At your solar plexus, imagine a golden yellow light filling your upper abdomen:

Say to yourself, 'I accept my power, my ability to succeed and my need to have some control over my life.'

At your heart centre, between your breasts, imagine a clear green light filling your chest and right down your arms to your fingertips:

Say to yourself, 'I accept myself totally, exactly as I am now. I am.'

At your throat, see a clear, sky-blue light filling your throat and extending to the tips of your ears, nose, mouth and jaw:

Say to yourself, 'I accept the way I express myself in the world. I accept my creative nature.'

At your brow, see a deep indigo blue light extending out to fill the rest of your head:

Say to yourself, 'I accept my wisdom, my understanding of reality.'

At the crown of your head imagine a clear violet light pouring out from the top of your head and dissolving into pure white light:

Say to yourself, 'I accept my divinity, my connection with cosmic, universal energy.'

Now imagine pure white light pouring into you through the crown of your head and breath it into the centre of your being on your in-breath and, on your out-breath, imagine that you are sending the light to every cell and atom of your body. See the whole of you, inside and out, radiant with the light; the life force energy. Continue to breath quietly and circulate the light for a few minutes.

Say to yourself, 'I am in the light and the light is in me.'*

With that under your belt, you might even be tempted to try working a little magic.

* Taken from *Crystals for Life* by Jacquie Burgess, New Leaf Books, Dublin, Ireland, 2000, by kind permission of the author.

23
The Secret Centres

You can get more information on the chakras at any yoga centre or any bookshop. But unless you meet a practising wizard, all you'll get is blank looks when you ask about the astro-mental centres.

Just as the chakras 'stand behind' various glands, nerve centres and organs in the physical body, the astro-mental centres 'stand behind' the chakras.

Just as the chakras influence physical processes, the astro-mental centres influence the chakras. Their very existence has been a secret taught only in the wizard lodges and a few rare books. The reason for the secrecy is that they can be used *directly* to work magic.

Although the secret centres seem to exist in a different reality, they do have specific locations within or close to your physical body.

Have a look at the following diagram:

ASTRO-MENTAL CENTRES

The first thing you'll notice is that there are only five astro-mental centres, whereas there are seven chakras. The next thing you'll notice is that while two of the centres – solar plexus and base – seem to coincide with chakras, the others don't. Two of them lie outside the body altogether, while the third seems to be centred *between* two chakras. In point of fact, none of the centres is located in your body at all. They're in your aura. Taken together, they're known to wizards as the Middle Pillar.

If you want to be an athlete, you train your body. If you want to be a wizard, you train your astro-mental centres. The first step is to make them active. Here's how:

Find somewhere you won't be disturbed, relax completely then visualise a sphere of brilliant white light hanging in space above the crown of your head. Vibrate the sounds *Eh-heh-yeh.*

(To vibrate a sound, you should pitch your voice a shade lower than you would normally use and let the word originate at the back of the throat. When you get it right, you'll feel the vibration. The sound itself, and the others you'll be using, are all ancient Hebrew names for God, in phonetic spelling. Even wizards who aren't Jewish use these sounds because they've discovered they work.)

If you visualise strongly and vibrate properly, you'll feel the effects at once. There's a surge of energy and a tingling sensation. If it doesn't happen, keep practising until it does.

Once you get the first sphere right, move on to the next. Visualise a shaft of brilliant white light moving downwards from the crown sphere through the centre of your skull and blossoming into a second sphere of white light at your throat. Vibrate the sounds *Yeh-ho-vo El-hoh-eem*.

Let the shaft of light continue down to your solar plexus region and produce a third sphere. Vibrate *Yeh-ho-vo-El-hoh-ah-vey-daas*.

Extend the shaft to your genitals where a fourth sphere is established to the sounds *Shad-ay-El-chay*.

Finally imagine the shaft continuing down to produce the fifth sphere at your feet. Vibrate *Ah-do-nay-ha-Are-etz* and contemplate the entire shaft of silvery light and the sparkling centres for a few moments, sensing the inflow of energy.

Practice the sequence twice a day, morning and evening, for at least a month; longer if you like. When you're happy with results, you can switch to the advanced exercise – the Middle Pillar visualised in colour:

Crown – White
Throat – Lavender
Solar Plexus – Red
Genitals – Blue
Feet – Russet

The shaft takes on the colour of the last sphere you visualise. In other words it starts as white, but after the throat sphere it turns lavender and so on.

When you've used the colour version of the Middle Pillar for at least three weeks and are really comfortable with it, you're ready for your first experiments in practical magic.

To start you off with something simple, why not charge the talisman you made after reading the chapter Creating a Soul-Stone. (You *did* make a talisman, didn't you?) Activate your Middle Pillar, circulate the energy, then saturate your aura with the negative colour associated with your planet. (See the table on page 262.)

Now all you have to do is visualise a ray of that colour streaming from your aura into the talisman. It only takes a few seconds before the talisman is fully charged. If you're any way sensitive, you'll be able to feel the difference the charge has made.

With that under your belt, you can go on to a more serious experiment in magic.

24
An Experiment in Magic

It's not like the panto where magic happens in a flash of light and puff of smoke. Every wizard worth his salt knows that real magic takes time and happens as if by coincidence. The trick is to trigger the coincidence. And the good news is you've already done most of the work by activating your Middle Pillar.*

To start your experiment, figure out what it is you want to do. Since this is your first time working real magic, I'd suggest you start small: you can leave winning the lottery or becoming dictator of the world until you get the hang of it… and learn there's always a price that has to be paid.

So what sort of thing should you aim for? Perhaps an exam success, a little money in your pocket, concert tickets, the recovery of

---

* If you *haven't* activated your Middle Pillar, go back and do the exercises now, otherwise you're wasting your time with the magical experiment.

something you've lost… things of this nature should be well within your reach, even as a beginner. Be specific. Target the actual examination, decide exactly *how much* money is 'a little'. Ideally, your goal should be something you might achieve by normal means if you put your mind to it and had a little luck. Remember this is only an experiment. But it's an important experiment, because success will lay a foundation for bigger things.

The system you're going to use to achieve your goal is very old indeed: the planetary associations that have formed the basis of astrology for generations. This form of magic dates to a time

PLANET	ASSOCIATIONS	POSITIVE COLOUR	NEGATIVE COLOUR
Sun	Life, growth, health, politics, power, success, money, superiors, mind power, spiritual illumination	Orange	Gold or Yellow
Mercury	Information, writing, Internet, broadcasting, contacts, trade, judgement, neighbours, books, short journeys	Yellow	Orange
Venus	Love, affection, emotion, pleasure, luxury, theatre, extravagance, art, beauty, self-indulgence	Emerald Green	Emerald Green
Moon	Creativity, women, childbirth, pregnancy, personality, change, the unconscious, psychism, imagination, hallucinations, witchcraft	Blue	Puce
Mars	Strength, power, vitality, willpower, charisma, destruction, danger, haste, anger, conflict, dominance	Bright Red	Bright Red
Jupiter	Prosperity, luck, expansion, banking, money, gambling, debtors, creditors, religion, visions, dreams, international travel	Purple	Blue
Saturn	Old age, cold, inertia, death, stability, stagnation, agriculture, land	Indigo	Black

when the sun and moon were thought of as planets and the only known planets were the ones you could see with the naked eye. Have a look at the table opposite and decide which planet best fits what you want to do.

You may find you have a choice of more than one planet. If your goal had to do with finance, for example, you'll note that money is associated both with the Sun and with Jupiter. Power is associated with both the Sun and Mars. In cases like this, you should make your choice based on the other associations listed for the planets concerned. If, for example, you wanted your money to come to you through luck, then your planet of choice would be Jupiter rather than the Sun. If you preferred it to result from your own efforts, your decision would be just the reverse.

You'll find two colours listed for each planet in the table – positive and negative. This has nothing to do with good and bad. The positive colour sends something away from you, the negative draws something towards you. Let's suppose you wanted your sister to get the broadcasting contract she was after. You'd pick the positive colour of Mercury because you want to send something out to another person. If, on the other hand, you wanted the contract yourself, you'd select the negative colour, because this would draw it towards you. (In two cases, Venus and Mars, positive and negative colours are both the same, so you have a very easy choice.)

With your goal set, your planet and colour chosen, you're ready to go.

An experienced wizard would take note of the cosmic tides that make it easier to work magic at certain times, but for the sake of simplicity you can ignore them in your first experiment. Start your operation on the first day of the month. Set aside fifteen minutes each morning and evening. Sit or lie down somewhere quiet, allow your body to relax completely, then activate your Middle Pillar exactly the way you learned in the last chapter.

Once you have the centres buzzing nicely, circulate the energy in the following way:

As you breathe in, visualise a sheet of white light emerging from the crown sphere above your head and travelling down the left side of your body. It should move just below your skin and leave a nice afterglow. Note with your mind's eye that the light is finally absorbed in the sphere at your feet.

Breathe out slowly.

On your next in-breath, visualise the light

travelling upwards from the foot sphere up the right side of your body until it is absorbed by the sphere above your head.

Breathe out slowly.

Repeat this circuit several times until you feel the effects, then set up a second circuit. For this one, the light travels down from the crown sphere over your face and down the front of your body where it is again absorbed by the foot sphere. On your next in-breath, let it travel up from the lower sphere along your back until it reaches the crown sphere again. Repeat this circuit several times as well.

The effect of this exercise is to charge your aura with an unusual type of energy. Your next step is to direct it.

So far, the circulating energy has been pure white light. Change that now to the colour associated with your goal. For the sake of an example, let's suppose your goal was to win £20 at bingo. Money, luck and gambling are all associated with Jupiter and the negative (attracting) colour of Jupiter is blue. So you would now begin to circulate a clear blue light throughout your aura. Visualise it strongly. Feel it soak into your very being until your whole aura glows with blue light.

Now picture the £20 clearly. See it *already in*

your possession. Imagine it is actually in your pocket right now. Know as a certainty you won it at bingo. Try to build a mindset of absolute confidence that your desired result has been achieved.

That's the magic in a nutshell, but there's one more thing you need to do. Wizards call it *opening the channels.* All it means is that you must act in a way *that allows the magic to work.* It's no use locking yourself in your room and waiting for results to drop through the ceiling – that's not working magic, it's asking for a miracle. If your goal is to win a competition, then you must enter competitions. If it's to find something you've lost, you must keep on looking for it. If you want to win £20 at bingo, then you must obviously get down to the village hall and *play* bingo.

Will the magic really work?

Try it.

Epilogue

The most famous source of information in the ancient world was the Library of Alexandria, in Egypt. It was founded by the Pharaoh at the beginning of the third century BC, built in the precincts of his palace at Brucheium and organised by Demetrius of Phaleron. A daughter library was established about 235 BC by Ptolemy III in the Temple of Sarapis.

Legend has it that the Library of Alexandria contained histories of the lost civilisation of Atlantis, details of marvellous inventions and the secrets of much dark wizardry. But the library was destroyed in a civil war that occurred under the Roman emperor Aurelian in the late third century AD and the daughter library was destroyed by Christians in AD 391, so no one can say for sure.

Or can they?

It is approaching midnight in the kitchen of a

267

remote farmhouse. Two wizards are engaged on a bizarre experiment. One is there purely as a troubleshooter and note-taker. If the experiment succeeds, the record of it must be preserved for others like them.

The second wizard has a much more active role, although at first glance you might be forgiven for missing it. She is slumped in her chair, eyes firmly closed. She looks asleep, but in fact she is in a deep trance. Subjectively, her mind is elsewhere.

She has been taken by Anubis, Ancient Egypt's spirit guardian of the dead, with whom she has a mystical affinity, to witness the destruction of the Library of Alexandria… and perhaps rescue one manuscript badly needed for her arcane studies.

'There is fighting in the streets,' she reports, her voice soft, but firm. 'The Roman soldiers are everywhere.'

Anubis guides her towards a young boy, perhaps sixteen or seventeen years old. He is running from the advancing troops, but Anubis seizes him. 'He will tell you how to reach the library,' the wizard says in the voice of Anubis. 'Question him!'

The note-taker begins to question the boy, now paralysed and fearful. He gives directions on how to reach the palace and the relevant buildings in the compound. He does not know what is happening to him. He is only aware of his inability to move and a voice that seems to emerge from the air beside his head.

Anubis releases him and he runs off. 'Will he be all right?' the entranced wizard asks quietly.

'He will die in twenty minutes when a Roman soldier finds him.'

The two wizards sigh in spontaneous sympathy for the boy. The clock in the farmhouse kitchen strikes midnight. Another day of wizardry has begun.

Acknowledgements

I've always been vaguely envious of authors who include pages of acknowledgements in their books: they all seem to have extensive research teams, personal assistants, secretaries and impressive contacts in exotic places. Most of my hundred or so books have been the result of my staring at a wall and occasionally logging onto the Internet.

But not this one. For this one I have a lot of people to thank.

First, the wizards of the Western Esoteric Tradition who have joined with me over the past forty years to experiment with a spiritual system that has never been popular with the public at large. Foremost among them must be my fellow author Dolores Ashcroft-Nowicki and my wife Jacks, who guided me through some interesting and difficult magical times, but the rosta has included professionals – lawyers, physicists, academics, engineers, several doctors and one judge – whose careers might well have suffered had their interest in wizardry become common knowledge. I salute their courage.

Next, Suzie Jenvey and Julia Wells of Faber who had the imagination and insight to commission a book like this and the good sense to let me get on with it without concerns about the political correctness of its subject matter.

Among those who contributed enormously to the book you hold now were Susan Reuben, my editor on the project, who displayed enormous attention to detail and ensured I retained clarity when attempting to describe the more obscure areas of my subject; Susan's dad, Dr Brian Posner, who worked unpaid for love of his daughter to set me right about the invisibility theories of H. G. Wells; Sophie Pelham, who burned the midnight oil to get the look and feel of the book as perfect as it has become; Ken de Silva, who created the magnificent cover that persuaded you to buy it; and Roisin Heycock, who guarded the sensitivities of you, the reader.

And finally, Stephanie von Reiswitz, whose illustrations have contributed so much to the overall impact and appearance of the work. I have already said it privately and will now repeat in print: Steph, I wish you'd been available to illustrate all my esoteric books.